Nat's blue eyes met his and John's train of thought was lost.

He liked watching the color creep into her cheeks and the spark ignite in those blue eyes—they went from sky blue to blazing sapphire in a matter of seconds.

All he had to do was lean in a couple of inches and his lips would meet hers. Every instinct told him to do it. He ached to do just that. To kiss her. Touch her. Breathe her in until he was lost in her. It'd be easy to do. And it would all start with one kiss...

One kiss and he'd ruin everything.

He couldn't afford to lose Nat. If he gave in to his craving for her, he'd never forgive himself. He didn't do relationships. Not romantically, anyway. He didn't have room for all the drama and complications, and damn it all, he didn't want drama and complications messing up what he and Nat had.

With Nat, he saw things differently. She gave him hope. Hope in life, in the future and in himself. And now hope that—maybe—he wasn't as hard and dried-up as he thought. Looking at Nat, his heart felt nothing but warmth and, yes, hope.

What the hell was he supposed to do with that?

Dear Reader,

If you've read either of the previous Texas Cowboys & K-9s books, you've met the Mitchell brothers before. All except one: John Mitchell. John's one of those complicated characters I love getting to know. His childhood was golden, but the loss of his father was the first of several hurts and betrayals. As a result, he has a hard time trusting people, himself included.

Natalie Harris, his best friend since childhood, is the exact opposite. Before she came to live with her grandfather, she'd spent most of her time alone, hungry and afraid. But coming to Granite Falls meant finding home, love and security. Having John back makes it perfect—if only he'd give his family and hometown a second chance.

Of course, things get more complicated when baby Leslie shows up—plus Vlad the one-eyed raccoon and trusty Alpha, the Labrador retriever, too. Needless to say, John and Nat have a lot to figure out before the story ends. I hope you'll be delighted with how things turn out.

Happy reading!

Sasha Summers

PS: Keep an eye out, I might have Vlad make a guest appearance in the next Granite Falls book.

The Rancher's Baby Surprise

SASHA SUMMERS

HARLEQUIN

SPECIAL
EDITION

HARLEQUIN®
SPECIAL EDITION™

Recycling programs
for this product may
not exist in your area.

ISBN-13: 978-1-335-40829-7

The Rancher's Baby Surprise

Copyright © 2021 by Sasha Best

This edition published by arrangement with Harlequin Books S.A.

For questions and comments about the quality of this book,
please contact us at CustomerService@Harlequin.com.

Harlequin Enterprises ULC
22 Adelaide St. West, 41st Floor
Toronto, Ontario M5H 4E3, Canada
www.Harlequin.com

Printed in U.S.A.

Sasha Summers grew up surrounded by books. Her passions have always been storytelling, romance and travel—passions she's used to write more than twenty romance novels and novellas. Now a bestselling and award-winning author, Sasha continues to fall a little in love with each hero she writes. From easy-on-the-eyes cowboys, sexy alpha-male werewolves, to heroes of truly mythic proportions, she believes that everyone should have their happily-ever-after—in fiction and real life.

Sasha lives in the suburbs of the Texas Hill Country with her amazing family. She looks forward to hearing from fans and hopes you'll visit her online: on Facebook at sashasummersauthor, on Twitter, @sashawrites, or email her at sashasummersauthor@gmail.com.

Books by Sasha Summers

Harlequin Special Edition

Texas Cowboys & K-9s

The Rancher's Forever Family
Their Rancher Protector

Harlequin Heartwarming

The Cowboys of Garrison, Texas

The Rebel Cowboy's Baby
The Wrong Cowboy

Visit the Author Profile page
at Harlequin.com for more titles.

For Chris,
thanks for keeping me grounded—no matter what.

Chapter One

"This is your last warning." Natalie Harris held her broom up, ready to defend herself if there was no other choice. "This is my house and my porch and my porch swing. You need to leave. Now." She shook the broom—pretty confident she wasn't pulling off the whole *menacing* thing.

The large raccoon, dubbed Vlad due to his underbite, yawned and slumped back in Nat's padded hammock chair.

So, not the least bit menacing. Great.

The raccoon stared at her with its one shiny black eye, showing no signs of concern… And no sign of moving, either.

"You're not fooling me." She advanced slowly, broom first. "I know you're scared of me." Maybe if she said it loud enough, they'd both believe her.

The raccoon scratched one ear with his back foot, leaning into the motion and closing his one good eye.

Or not.

"Come on, Vlad. I've had a long day." She sighed,

more pleading as she stepped closer, within broom reach now. "A long, long day. I want to sit on my porch, drink my tea and relax." If she was going to come up with a way to save the Bear's House, she needed a spark of genius. Right now, she wasn't feeling it. She tapped the straw bristles on the deck before the hammock swing.

Vlad sat forward, stared her in the eye and growled.

Natalie stopped. They both knew she wouldn't use the broom. They both knew she'd wind up in her rickety rocking chair while he sprawled on the comfy cushions of her new and barely used—by her, anyway—hammock swing.

"Vlad, can you give me the slightest break?" Everything about this was ridiculous. Who attempted negotiations with a massive, one-eyed, battle-scarred raccoon? Why not swat at him with the broom, shout and yell and claim what was hers?

Vlad sat back, blinked, rubbed his hands over his face, then rolled into a ball.

Natalie sighed, resting the broom against the mint-green staggered shake-style paneling covering her house. She didn't have enough energy for this. She could enjoy her tea in Grampa Bear's rocking chair. It was the same porch, the same view—if a little less comfy. What mattered was coming up with a plan. A doable plan. *I can do this*. But that didn't stop her from leaning forward and glaring at the raccoon that refused to back down. "You're lucky I'm so tired, Vlad…" The sentence hung in the air, lacking any real threat.

Vlad didn't even twitch in acknowledgment.

"Since you've named him, I'm thinking he has the upper hand." A deep voice floated across her front lawn, startling her just enough to knock the broom over and send Vlad scurrying off the porch and into the nearest tree, hissing and growling as he went.

I know that voice. Her heart stopped. *Please. Please.* Was he home? *Finally?* Natalie turned, peering into the twilight, unexpectedly nervous and over-the-moon delighted. "John?"

"Hey, Nat."

It is *him.* His was her favorite voice in the whole wide world.

"John?" she repeated, stunned. *He's really, truly here?*

"Am I welcome?" he asked. "Or do I need to worry about the assassin-broom action you've got going on?" He opened the white picket gate and came inside, a large black Labrador trailing after him.

"You're welcome," she said, laughing. She hadn't realized she was running, and her arms slid around his neck, knocking his cowboy hat to the ground. It was the only way to know she wasn't imagining this. He was big and warm, wrapping her up in a hug.

He chuckled, lifted her up and spun her around. "No broom, then?" He sighed, tightening his hold.

"It's too early to say, yet. Just know I have it and I'm not afraid to use it." She eased out of his hold, eager to look at him. "Come in. Sit. When did you get back? Are you hungry? Thirsty? I have iced tea? Or a beer, I think?" She picked up his cowboy hat, dusted it off and handed it to him.

"Thanks." John took the hat. "A beer would be great."

"What about your friend? Is he or she a beer drinker?" She crouched in front of the Labrador, noting the white and gray dusting the dog's muzzle and around its eyes. "Hello," she said, offering her hands up in greeting. The dog obligingly sniffed, then gave her a slow tail wag.

"Alpha is a straight-vodka drinker. But he's trying to break the habit, so water would be good." John chuckled.

Nat shot him a look. "I'll make sure to remember that. No vodka for you." She gave the dog a scratch behind the ear. "You are the biggest Lab I have ever seen, Alpha."

"He's big and loyal and has one intimidating bark, but he's harmless." John patted the dog on the back. "He and Vlad will probably be braiding each other's hair pretty quick."

She cradled Alpha's face in her hands. "I wouldn't bet on it. Vlad's not exactly the braid-your-hair type. I'd steer clear of him if I was you."

Alpha seemed unconcerned, his dark brown eyes on her face and his long black tail still wagging slowly.

She stood and stared up at John. "I can't believe you're here." She'd missed him. "How long are you home for?"

"For good." His lips tightened. "Plenty of time for catching up…and a few beers, too."

She nodded, beyond thrilled that he was home… but worried about the reason behind it. John's plan had been to be a military man. He'd wanted to put in his twenty years and retire. He'd only been gone for eight years. Eight years, ten months and seventeen days—not that she was keeping track. Her gut had told her something had happened when his letters had gotten further and further apart. She hadn't heard a word from him in months, and now, all of a sudden, he was here. *Something has happened, all right.* Nat knew John, knew he wasn't one to give up without a fight… *Unless he had no choice.*

Until they reached the stairs, Natalie hadn't noticed his limp. Then it was obvious. From the way he stepped and leaned out: his left knee was bothering him. It took effort to manage the three steps up and onto her porch, a lot of effort. Was this why he was home? Had he been injured? Question after question bubbled up, but she managed to hold back. He didn't acknowledge his injury, and she wouldn't, either. Not yet, anyway. John would tell her when he was ready; he told her everything. Normally. Then again, he hadn't told her he was heading home…

John glanced at Grampa Bear's empty rocking chair, his hand coming up to rest along the curved wicker back. How many hours had they spent here, she, John and Grampa Bear? How many memories had been made on this porch? She saw his fingers grip the chair for a moment, his jaw clenched tight, before his gaze met hers.

She swallowed hard, a massive lump lodging in her throat. Losing Grampa Bear… She shook her head, hoping he'd understand. She didn't like to talk about Grampa Bear's death. Not yet. It had been years, but it was still so raw. Besides, she'd rather focus on John—to be happy and celebrate his homecoming. She took a deep breath and forced the words out. "You can take Vlad's spot," she suggested, the slight waver in her voice revealing too much.

Thankfully, John nodded and let it go.

The white Christmas lights she kept tacked along the inside of the porch roof shed just enough light to really see John. He wore what he always wore. A button-down blue plaid shirt, on the threadbare side. Worn jeans. The same cowboy boots and straw cowboy hat he'd been wearing when he left. There were dark bags under his eyes, a hollowness to his cheeks and a thick scar that ran along his left temple, down his cheek and neck to disappear under the stretched-out neckline of his black T-shirt. He looked tired, the kind of tired that it would take time to recover from. John needed to rest and, from the looks of it, some healing, too. She drew in a deep breath. Between her, his mother and brothers, he'd have support and love and peace and quiet—just what he needed. He was home now. *For good.*

"You weren't planning on sitting there?" he asked, ending her mental musings.

"No, no. Company first. You go right ahead. At this point, I should order another one, give up the fight." She peered into the tree Vlad had retreated into.

Vlad hissed at her.

"What fun would that be?" John asked. "It is Granite Falls, after all."

She didn't miss the hint of scorn to his voice. She'd hoped that, after leaving home, he'd come to appreciate their hometown. Yes, it was small, everyone knew everyone else's business, and the day-in-and-day-out sort of living was at a less-than-brisk pace. But those were the very things Nat had loved about Granite Falls. When she'd come to live here with her grandfather Barron Harris, Bear to friends and family, she'd been hungry for people who would care about her—care enough to make sure she was safe, had three meals a day and a roof over her head. Grampa Bear had done just that.

And I won't forget it. That's why, after John left, she'd get back to figuring out how to keep the Bear's House Bar and BBQ. It'd been Grampa Bear's baby for…well, forever. Now, it was Nat's. She had to hold on to it. The Bear's House wasn't just a place and a job, it was Nat's second home, and the patrons and staff were like family. Even though running the Bear's House was all-consuming, losing the place, after losing Grampa Bear, was too much to consider. *It won't happen. I won't let it happen.*

"A standoff with a raccoon sounds pretty eventful for these parts. Might even be able to sell tickets." John winked her way, snapping her back to the present.

She smiled. She had to. That was the thing about John: when he wanted to be charming, there was *no one* more charming than he was.

She'd moved here two years before John's father passed, and those two years were enough for her to irrevocably hand over her heart to John Henry Mitchell. John's childhood had been far more golden than hers. By all appearances, he had no reason for lingering hostility. A big and loving family, wealth, a known and respected name. But after John's father died, the Mitchell world was forever changed. John lashed out at everyone—her included. And while it was understandable that he was hurting, he refused to let anyone comfort him. Instead, he had mastered the art of verbal warfare. His words had become hate-filled missiles lobbed far and wide, fired at anyone within John's line of vision. Once he'd started, there was no stopping him. John's charm and zest for life had gone hard, twisting up his insides and making him angry with life. He seemed hell-bent on pushing the limits, taking risks and not caring about the consequences.

And through it all, Nat had watched and loved him. He was her friend. Even at his worst, she knew he'd needed her. Nat knew the pain that came from being discarded by those who mattered most, and she wouldn't do that to John. She believed, somehow—someway—John would find his way back. He'd look around him and see things without all the hate clouding his vision. Until then, she'd let him sit in her hammock chair, give him a beer and be there for him—no matter what.

John could feel Nat's eyes on him. She had questions for him. Of course she did. But, knowing Nat, she'd wait for him to start the conversation.

That's not gonna happen.

The last thing he wanted to do was talk about his knee, his scars or anything too heavy. He'd spent the last ten months trying to figure out what his life would look like now that he'd been discharged from the Marines. He hadn't told his family—hell, anyone—about his injury or his discharge, so going home hadn't been an option. He'd put his family through enough; he hadn't wanted to add to that by worrying them. But the more he and Alpha had driven back and forth across the country looking for answers, the more lost and alone he'd felt.

When he'd made his weekly check-in call, his mother had told him his brother Kyle was getting married. And just like that, John had headed home.

Showing up was bound to be a surprise. A good one, he hoped. *But I guess we'll see what Hayden has to say about that.*

As much as he dreaded another run-in with his older brother, there was no denying he was happy to be home. The rugged beauty of the rolling hills, the familiar scenery and faces, from the fresh peaches hanging low on the trees to the constant symphony of crickets, cicadas and doves, eased some of the ache he'd carried since he'd first set foot on American soil as a civilian. Sure, it was hot—it was Texas, after all—but the heat didn't get to him. He'd always preferred being outdoors to indoors. The last few years had taught him he preferred quiet to conversation, and for the most part, he preferred being alone to keeping company.

Natalie Harris was the exception. Nat had always had a sort of sixth sense about him. She seemed to know what he wanted and needed before he did, and she always—*always*—saw right through him. Right now, that's exactly what he needed. No pressure, no expectations and no answers... Not right now, anyway. He'd deal with Hayden and his family tomorrow.

Alpha yawned, stretched and flopped onto the wide wooden porch. "Make yourself at home," Nat said, smiling. She glanced his way. "You both look tired."

John tried to lower himself into the hammock swing like it wasn't a big deal. He was just sitting down—it *shouldn't* be a big deal. And, if it wasn't for his leg, it wouldn't be a big deal. But his knee was a patched-together mess, and his range of motion would never resemble anything normal, so he had to make do. There was no way he was going to let a little discomfort affect his daily life. He locked his jaw, sat and swallowed the grunt of discomfort that stung at the back of his throat. As soon as he was seated, he stretched both of his legs out in front of him to alleviate the stress.

With any luck, a few beers would take the edge off the pain.

He glanced up to find Nat, her hands clasped

in front of her, smiling at him like he was Santa Claus.

"I can't believe you're here." She shook her head. "I'm *so* glad you're here."

He nodded, pushed his cowboy hat back on his head and smiled in return. Nat just had one of those smiles, irresistible. She always had. That hadn't changed. But now that he was sitting still and there was enough light to see clearly, he got an eyeful. Of Nat. But what he saw? Well, she was a bit of a shock. A *whole* lot had changed.

When he'd left, he'd been a mess of a hotheaded twenty-year-old, and Nat had been all tomboy, with long braids, shapeless denim overalls and a feisty attitude. Sure, they'd had a few FaceTime calls and he'd seen her once on leave for a couple of hours a few years back, but he was pretty sure she hadn't looked like this *then*. Maybe he hadn't been paying attention?

This Nat didn't have braids. Her dark hair was cut along her jawline, sleek and glossy and sweeping down and across her forehead at an angle. Her nails were painted, and she wore dangling earrings. Not so tomboy, either. But the most worrisome difference was the lack of denim overalls. Why did she have to look so…womanly? This was Nat. *Nat* Nat. She'd never been a small woman that poked at her food, but he'd never noticed—or cared—about her figure. Now it was impossible to miss. This Nat was all curves and femininity. Any man would be hard-pressed not to notice— and appreciate…

These were not the sort of thoughts he wanted to have when he was thinking about Nat. She was his friend. Little things like her rear or the way her red shirt cupped and clung to places he didn't want to notice needed to stop. "It's been a while, Nat." Not exactly a great conversation starter, but true nonetheless.

"A couple of years." She nodded.

He regretted not making more trips to Granite Falls when he had leave. But, being the stubborn ass he was, he'd thought he was making some sort of point. Instead, he'd lost, forever, time with a man he'd loved.

"Let me get you and Alpha your drinks. Give me a sec." She held up one finger and opened the screened front door, letting it slam behind her.

He waited. He could almost hear Bear Harris snap at her for *making all that racket*. Bear Harris had been a good, salt-of-the-earth man who loved his motorcycles, his military models, the Bear's House Bar and BBQ and his granddaughter. He'd been a little rough around the edges, but John had always known where he stood with Bear, and John had respected that. He'd respected Bear, period.

"You'd have liked Bear," he said to Alpha, giving the dog's neck a firm rub. "He was good people." And sitting here, on his porch, without hearing Bear bellowing about Nat slamming around in the kitchen felt wrong. Until now, he hadn't thought about how alone and isolated Nat was. *Because I'm a selfish ass.* He ran a hand over his face, hating himself all over again.

Nat emerged seconds later, a longneck beer in one hand and a large ceramic mixing bowl painted with daisies in the other. The bowl was so full, water sloshed over the rim.

"Gentlemen," she said, bending to place the bowl on the ground next to Alpha. "Refills are on the house." She gave Alpha a quick pat, then stood and offered John the ice-cold beer.

"Nothing for you?" John asked.

She pointed at the tall glass of iced tea and frowned. "I had my beverage of choice…and then Vlad showed up—"

"Right." John chuckled. "That was some showdown."

"He's quite a character." But Nat didn't seem all that upset over the supersized, belligerent raccoon. Then again, she was alone so, belligerent or not, Vlad was company for her.

"How are you doing?" The question was out before he could stop it. So much for steering clear of all serious topics of conversation. He hadn't even made it fifteen minutes.

Nat glanced at him, crossing the porch to grab

the arm of the old wooden rocking chair and drag it closer to the swing. "Fine." She sat, cradling her glass of iced tea.

He didn't buy it. At all. The way she pulled herself up, curling in on herself in that chair told him otherwise. And it was a gut punch. One that took a minute to recover from. "I'm sorry I wasn't here…" He leaned forward, ignoring the sharp tug behind his knee.

"You sent flowers," she sniffed, taking the hand he offered. "From wherever you were serving. I bet that couldn't have been easy." She squeezed his hand before letting go. "It was peaceful… He just didn't wake up." She sipped her watered-down tea. "I went in with his coffee, to let him know he was running behind…" She shrugged. "No illness or injury or pain. There's some comfort in that."

For Nat, maybe. John suspected Bear would have preferred to raise some hell to the end. But John kept that to himself. He'd been gone too long to know how Bear would or wouldn't have felt anymore. "I'm sorry. Damn sorry. He was one of a kind."

"He was." She leaned forward to peer up into the tree at the edge of the porch. "Vlad showed up a few weeks after Bear's passing. I don't know if he'd always been here and was too scared of Bear to make himself known or if Bear sent him to keep me company. The raccoon is just as surly as Bear ever was." She shot John a glance. "That's probably why I can't bring myself to trap him."

John leaned back in the chair, smiling. He didn't hold much faith in the idea that the dead looked out for the living. In his experience, death was just death. The end. The person was gone—taking all the things left unsaid and undone to haunt the ones left behind. But if Nat needed to think that Bear had sent some oversize rodent to keep her company, he wouldn't ruin it for her. Bear hadn't just been her grandfather, he'd been her *only* relative. Losing him meant Nat was alone.

Another gut punch. This one was harder and weighted with a good amount of guilt.

"You sell the Bear's House?" he asked, suspecting he already knew the answer. The Bear's House Bar and BBQ had been a long-standing institution in Granite Falls. Bear's motorcycle-loving friends tended to show up in groups, lining the far end of Main Street and causing all sorts of complaints from the more tightly laced residents.

"No." Nat looked horrified. "Never." She made a weird-pitched sound, half shock and half disbelief. "Of course not."

"I figured as much." John chuckled. "You're running the place, then?" Considering she'd spent just as much time there as she had at home, it made sense.

She nodded. "Bear only hired loyal people, you

know that. I'm just lucky they stayed once he—" She broke off to take a deep breath. "Having them means I don't have to live, sleep and breathe the place." She leaned toward him, confessing, "Of course, I *am* still there every day." Her blue gaze swept over his face slowly, searching, before she sat back in the rocking chair and stared out into the darkness.

Hell… He blinked, forcing his eyes from her profile to the beer in his hands. After being gone for almost nine years, of course, there'd been some changes. In his mind, though, he always pictured Nat the same—unchanged. But the hair and the jewelry and the eyes and the clothes… It was going to take some time to get his mind wrapped around this Nat. Appearances aside, he was grateful that Nat was still Nat. His friend, the person he could count on through anything—no matter what.

It'd been a long time since he'd been back to Granite Falls, and he didn't know where he *fit*. Tomorrow he'd go home, to the ranch, and see what sort of greeting he'd get. As much as he'd like to think they'd welcome him with open arms, he wasn't about to hold his breath. At least, where Hayden was concerned. John had said some horrible things before he left, doing his best to wound his big brother. He might not have wanted to see it then, but he'd come to terms with his part in their falling-out. His was the lion's share. It was long past time for John to own up to that and apologize.

Would Hayden accept? Would he be willing to set aside the old wounds or would he get all smug and push back at John? Hayden had warned John his temper would hurt him, and, boy, had he called it. That was exactly what had happened. John's temper had cost him his knee, his military career and his future. John had to live with that.

Whether he and Hayden liked one another didn't really matter. They were brothers, and they needed to clear the air. It wouldn't be easy. John feared Hayden would use that condescending voice of his or launch into an *I told you so* speech and John's temper would, once more, get the better of him. But, and it was a big *but*, if there was a chance he and his brother could come to some sort of understanding, it would be worth it. At least that's what John kept telling himself.

"You okay with Alpha and me staying here tonight?" he asked. "It's awful late to surprise my family. But tomorrow... I figure it can wait one more night." Truth be told, he needed one more night before facing his mother and brothers.

"As long as you'd like." Nat didn't hesitate. "There's plenty of room."

"I appreciate it." He could breathe.

Her blue eyes met his, steady and warm. "You're always welcome, John. Don't you know that?"

He nodded. "But it's nice to hear." Depending on how tomorrow played out, he might need a place to stay. "That means a lot, Nat."

"You and Alpha put your feet up and rest awhile." She smiled.

He was tired. So damn tired. Tired of aimless wandering and tired of avoiding what needed doing. Tomorrow, he'd change that. Tomorrow, he'd find out if there was a place for him on the family ranch or if there was no repairing the damage he'd left behind.

Chapter Two

Nat poured a cup of coffee and slid it across the wooden tabletop. "Milk or sugar or creamer?"

John shook his head. "Black. Thanks, Nat."

"How did you sleep?" she asked, whisking some cinnamon into the egg-and-milk French toast batter.

"Like a log." John sat back, stretching his legs out with a wince, before looking her way.

"Alpha sleep okay?" she asked. "I checked. No missing vodka this morning."

John chuckled. "That's good. He doesn't let the lack of opposable thumbs slow him down—much."

There was nothing like seeing John Mitchell smile. Maybe it wasn't a big smile, the sort of carefree, dimpled, charming smile that used to make her heart trip over itself, but it was still a smile. "He might not have helped himself to the vodka, but he did something last night." She nodded at the dog, sprawled out and sleeping in the middle of the tiled kitchen floor.

John smiled at the snoring dog. "More like he's just enjoying retirement to the fullest."

Nat dunked a slice of thick bread in the batter and put it on the butter coated skillet. "How did the two of you meet up?" As far as she knew, John hadn't had a canine with him in action.

"Through a mutual friend." He turned his coffee mug. "Alpha and I only paired up after I got stateside. He was a bomb-sniffer, but he'd retired with his handler, a buddy of mine, a few years back." He sipped his coffee. "Ty. Good man. Barely retired and drops dead from pancreatic cancer. After the funeral, this old man had no place to go, so Alpha and I decided we'd keep each other company from here on out. I couldn't stand by and see Alpha packed off to some shelter. He's a veteran, after all."

"No, no way." Nat stared down at Alpha, still snoring. "The way you two are together, I'd assumed you'd been together for…a long time." She frowned when she thought of where Alpha could have ended up. "Glad you gave the old guy a home." She flipped the French toast.

"It's not easy." John sighed. "You can see how high-maintenance he is."

Nat laughed then. "I do see." She slid three pieces of French toast onto a plate and carried it to him. "Let me get the syrup."

"This looks great, Nat." He eyed the plate with appreciation. "A lot better than the last meal you cooked for me."

Nat spun around. "I can't believe you remember that." She shrugged and carried the syrup to the table. "I meant well. I was trying to be thoughtful."

"I appreciated the thought. The chipped tooth? Not so much." He took the syrup. "Thank you."

"Chipped tooth," Nat snorted. "You did not chip your tooth on my waffles."

"We'll have to agree to disagree on that one." John winked at her, pouring syrup all over his French toast.

She served herself and carried her plate to the table, sitting across from him. "Whatever." She rolled her eyes. "What time are you expected out at the ranch?" Not that she was in a hurry to see him go.

He paused, his fork halfway to his mouth. "No set time."

"I bet they're excited." She cut into her toast. "Your mom must be on cloud nine."

John made a noncommittal sound.

It wasn't the first time she'd heard him make that sound. It was his *I don't want to talk about it* sound. Considering he hadn't been home in some time, it wasn't the reaction she'd expected. Things were strained between him and Hayden, she knew that, but not enough that they wouldn't all celebrate his homecoming, surely? From the corner of her eye, she watched him poke at his food until she couldn't take it any longer. "I can come with you, if you want."

John sat his fork down, his jaw muscle taut.

"Or not," she murmured, cutting off another piece of toast and taking a bite.

His gaze bounced from her to his coffee. "They're not exactly expecting me."

He looked and sounded so vulnerable, her heart twisted in on itself. "They'll be happy to see you, John." She gave him what she hoped was a reassuring smile.

He made that noise again.

"They will." She pushed. It was on the tip of her tongue to tell him that, over the years, Hayden had often come by the Bear's House just to see if she'd heard anything from John. Whatever had happened between them, Hayden loved his little brother. But Grampa Bear told her time and time again to stay out of other people's business. Instead, she said, "I know they will." Besides, her job was to have John's back.

He shrugged.

If he didn't want to talk, fine. But maybe she could set him at ease a little. "You'll like Hayden's wife, Lizzie," she said, cutting off another bite of toast. "Now, *she* is a cook. I don't know how she stays so slim. She teaches out at the new high school. Art." She paused, happy to see he was eating again. "And Skylar, Kyle's fiancée, is a veterinary technician. She works with Buzz over at the animal hospital."

John looked at her then. "How is ol' Buzz?" He scooped up a bite. "You two still dating?"

Nat rolled her eyes again. That had been over for almost a year now. Not that the two of them had ever been serious. "Nope." She sighed. "Buzz is... well, he's Buzz. In the end, we're best as friends." When she looked his way, he was watching her. No, more like studying her. "What's that look for?"

He shoved a massive bite of toast in his mouth and shook his head.

"Okay." She took a sip of her coffee. "And Skylar's kids... Oh, John—" She broke off, shaking her head. "They are the sweetest girls. Kyle adores them."

John smiled, mopping up the syrup with his last bite of French toast.

"No tooth-cracking this time?" she asked.

He held up one finger, finished chewing and swallowed. "Wanted to finish before I said one way or the other." He ran his tongue over his teeth and nodded. "All good."

She laughed. "I'm so glad."

"That was really good, Nat. I appreciate the food." He stood, carrying his plate to the sink. "And the bed." He glanced her way. "And for you...being you."

She had to smile at that. "Who else would I be?"

He rinsed off the plate.

"You don't have to do that." She carried her now-empty plate to the sink, took his and shooed him away. "Let me take care of you for a bit. I get the feeling no one's taken care of you in a while."

The corner of his mouth cocked up. "A while." He ran a hand along the nape of his neck and leaned back against the kitchen counter. "I don't want to take advantage is all."

"I'll let you know," Nat promised, rinsing off the plates and loading them into the dishwasher.

"You working?" he asked, his gaze settling on the large clock.

She nodded. "But not until later." She wiped her hands on the kitchen towel. "So…if you do want me to go with you, I can."

He seemed to consider her offer but wound up shaking his head again. "I think it's best if I do this on my own." He sounded calm, but there was tension rolling off him.

Poor John. She leaned against the counter beside him, nudging him. "It's going to be okay, John. It's going to be more than okay. I promise."

He looked down at her, his brown eyes searching hers. "Be careful making promises you can't keep, Nat."

That look, that tone, was new. This was a side of John she hadn't seen. Closed off and hard and out of reach. "I'm sorry, John." She covered her hand with his. "If I said or did something—"

"No." He shook his head, his smile tight. "You didn't do a thing, Nat. I guess I just…woke up on the wrong side of the bed."

If they hadn't been laughing a few minutes before, she might have believed him. But his mood had taken a nosedive once they'd started talking about his family. Whether he admitted it or not, this reunion was weighing on him. "*If* things go sideways, come to the Bear's House. Drinks are one me." She nudged him again.

He nudged her back. "Deal." With a sigh and another look at the clock, he pushed off the counter. "Thanks again. For…everything."

For a split second, Nat caught a flash of fear and uncertainty and anxiety streak across his handsome face. That was all it took for her to wrap her arms around him. "My pleasure," she murmured against his chest.

His arms were iron bands around her waist. Strong and warm and solid.

It felt good to be held. No, he felt good. And oddly disconcerting. "I'm so glad I didn't break any more of your teeth," she teased, staring up into those brown eyes until Nat was wrapped up in a bone-deep warmth.

John had a hard time meeting Nat's gaze. It had been a long time since someone had looked at him without any sort of skepticism or disappointment.

Nat never saw him that way. Even now, after years apart, her eyes were full of…faith. But in what, exactly? Him? That everything would work out with his family today? Whatever it was, he wanted her to be right.

Even with the impending morning's events, there was part of him entirely focused on the here and now. As in, here, hugging this new womanly version of Nat, in Bear's kitchen, and how none of it was the way it should be. Specifically, that he was aware of just how…womanly Nat felt in his arms. Very aware. *Too aware.* He was in no way prepared for how soft and warm and entirely too feminine she was. It wasn't so much bad as *different*. Especially the urge to tuck a strand of her cropped and sassy hair behind her ear, the way she seemed to prefer it. *What the hell is wrong with me?* This was Nat, for crying out loud. He wasn't about to derail a lifelong friendship because his sleep-deprived brain was confused and…*aware*. Still, this hugging thing wasn't helping. "I should go." He stepped back.

Nat nodded, her gaze sweeping over his face as she reached up to tuck the hair behind her ear. A sparkly star swung from a long golden hoop, drawing his gaze to her ear and neck and…

Dammit. He swallowed against the tightening of his throat.

"Well, give your mom my best." She turned.

"Wait, here." She opened the pantry and pulled out a jar. "Strawberry jam. Only a few jars left, but I know how much your mom loves it."

John looked at the jam jar. "Nat, you don't have to—"

"Oh, right." She frowned and sat the jar on the counter. "I guess… I guess they don't know you spent the night here?"

He grabbed the jar. "I don't give a damn about that, Nat. But you don't have to—"

"I want to." She smiled.

He nodded. "I'll see you later." After he'd caught some shut-eye and closed down this whole bizarre Nat-reaction thing. And after he'd dealt with his family. His brother. *I need more coffee.* He whistled, rousing Alpha from his comfy spot on the floor. "You ready, old man?"

Alpha stretched and yawned before his tail wagged.

"I'll see you two later?" Nat followed them to the front door. "Not later today, of course. But… later." She blew out a slow breath. "I guess I sort of worry this isn't real and you're going to up and disappear on me." There was a slight waver to her voice.

He paused, noting the slightest tightening of her big blue eyes. She'd been on her own too long— he'd played a part in that. Hayden wasn't the only one he'd wronged. He needed to make things right with her, too. He swallowed down the self-loathing and murmured, "I'm not going anywhere, Nat." He hurried to add, "I mean, that's not my plan."

"But if your plan changes, you'll let me know—in person—before you leave?" Her smile faltered.

He nodded, unable to stop himself from reaching up and tucking the strands behind her ear again. His fingertips brushed along the curve of her ear and cheek. "I promise."

"Good." She sighed, blinking rapidly.

He nodded again, turned on his heel and walked out the front door, his fingers tingling. *That was a mistake.* But he sure as hell wasn't going to overthink things. He was out of sorts for a hell of a lot of reasons, none of which had to do with Nat. Once those were squared away, things would be back to normal with Nat. It made sense. *Sounds good.* So, for now, Nat and his haywire response to her had to wait.

He followed Alpha down the flagstone path and across the dead-end street to the Jeep he'd inherited from Ty—along with Alpha. He opened the door and gave Alpha a boost, suspecting the step up took a toll on the dog's joints. Not that Alpha complained. He was all soulful eyes, tail wags and appreciative grunts. As far as John was concerned, Alpha was the damn-perfect traveling companion and dog.

Nat's place was on the outskirts of one side of

Granite Falls, and the Mitchell ranch was a few miles on the other side, which meant he caught a glimpse of the little town waking up. Both the coffee shop and diner were packed with breakfast-goers, a group of silver-haired matrons were speed-walking down Main Street and school buses were picking up students.

"This is Granite Falls, Alpha," he said, patting the Labrador on the shoulder. "Not much of a tour, I know. But I think you'll like the ranch. It's got a big back porch, perfect for long naps."

The closer they got to the ranch, the more on edge he felt.

"It is what it is," he mumbled. Maybe he should have brought a white flag? He didn't know what sort of greeting he was going to get, but he wasn't going to let that stop him from apologizing or saying all the things that needed to be said. Finally.

He pulled up in front of the ranch house—unchanged—and parked the Jeep in the shade of a massive oak tree. He should move, do something, but he sat frozen until Alpha licked his ear. "Yeah, yeah." He reached up and scratched the dog. "I'm going." He stepped down from the Jeep, rolled its side flaps up so the cool morning breeze kept the temperature pleasant and poured water into the bowl for Alpha. He took a deep breath. "I'll be back in a few."

Alpha yawned and flopped across the back seat, stretching.

"Glad to see you're not worried." *That makes one of us.* He walked to the porch and took the steps two at a time, ignoring the pull in his knee. But then he stopped, staring at the thick wooden front door. Was he supposed to knock and wait? No. This was his home. He knocked, but then he opened the door and stepped inside the home he'd grown up in.

"Hello?" His gaze swept the empty great room and landed on the kitchen table. His mother sat, reading glasses perched on the end of her nose, scanning a newspaper. He took a moment to get a good look at her. Nat might look like a different person, but his mother hadn't changed a bit. Seeing her tugged at something inside his chest. He'd missed her. So much. She was so absorbed in whatever she was reading, she hadn't heard him. "Mom?"

Her head popped up, and she pulled off her reading glasses. "John?" she whispered. "John Henry?" She stood slowly, dazed, bracing her hands on the table top.

"It's me." He didn't have to move, she was running toward him.

"Oh, my baby." She hugged him tight. "You're home? When did you get home? How are you? Let me look at you." She held him away from her, scanning him from head to toe.

"I'm fine," John assured her, smiling down at her.

But she ignored him and leaned close, her brow furrowing as her gaze traveled over his scars. "You're okay?"

"A little worse for wear. But all in one piece." Josh shrugged, trying to brush off her concern.

"I'm so glad." She was hugging him again.

It didn't matter how old he got: there was something almost medicinal in his mother's hug. Not that she could kiss it and make it all better—he'd outgrown that years ago. But knowing that, whatever happened, he had her support worked, too. Right now, he needed that. It might have taken him a long time to realize how blessed he was to have her—and his family—but he'd never forget it or take them for granted again.

"Do your brothers know?" she asked, pulling her cell phone from her pocket. "That you are home, I mean?"

"No." He shook his head. "I guess I thought surprising y'all would be a good idea." More like, he'd hoped the element of surprise would buy him the time to get it all out without interruption.

"Hayden?" his mother said into the phone. "Are you still at the barn or have you ridden out? Is Kyle with you?"

"Are they still at the barn?" John whispered.

She nodded. "I have news. About John."

"Wait." He held up his hand. "I'll go down to the barn."

She covered the phone. "You sure?"

He nodded.

"No…no…" his mother said into the phone. "Just, well…we can talk later." She frowned. "Be nice."

John was already heading across the great room, out the back door and along the path that led to the horse barn. Had it always been this far away from the house? Then again, last time he'd made the trek his left leg was fully functional. He needed to get better about the exercises his physical therapist had taught him in rehab. He'd never get full range of motion back, but the regimen should help with the stiffness and pain. By the time he reached the barn, his knee wasn't the only thing throbbing. His poor heart was pounding against his rib cage. His nerves were strung tight, and his lungs burned for air. All that compounded when he saw Hayden and Kyle, inside the barn, sliding bags of feed into the bed of the ranch pickup truck. He paused, just outside the door, to steady himself and clear his head.

"What do you think the news is? About John?" he heard his brother Kyle say, the *thunk* of a feed bag hitting the truck bed. "Poor Mom misses John something fierce, worries about him."

"He's given her plenty to worry about." Hayden's tone was hard. "I keep thinking he'll realize how tough this is on her, on all of us, but I should know better by now."

John flinched but knew Hayden was right.

"How long has it been since you've heard from him?" Kyle asked.

"Me?" Hayden snorted. "He does his best not to talk to me at all. But the last few months, he's gone longer and longer between calls with Mom. Of course, she *did* give him an earful about his latest disciplinary action."

John nodded, remembering all too well. An *earful* was an understatement. His mother had been so livid over his latest bout of insubordination that he'd barely gotten a word in edgewise before their time was up. That all seemed so long ago. Hayden was right about the phone calls, too. Since becoming a civilian, he'd lost track of time and missed a weekly call or two. Or more.

"John's never been a fan of lectures." Kyle chuckled. "Who is?"

"Or taking orders, either, apparently." Hayden made an impatient sound. "He keeps going off, half-cocked and fuming, and that will end his military career. It's just a matter of time. Then what? He comes back here to pick fights and let me know—every second of every day—that I'm not our father?" He sighed.

"Maybe not." Kyle didn't sound all that hopeful.

"Maybe," Hayden agreed. "But hating me was

a full-time job for John. I don't see how that will have changed."

John's chest felt weighted, pressing in until it hurt to breathe.

"I can't go back and erase what's been done and said between us, Kyle." Hayden's voice was hard. "I wish I could, believe me."

John had pushed his big brother, forcing Hayden to become the father figure and then hating him for it. He couldn't remember everything that had been said that last fight, but he remembered enough. John had wanted to wound Hayden. He'd wanted to leave his brother hurting while he went off to become a hero. That's why he was here, to apologize.

"I didn't want him enlisting, but once he did, I hoped it'd teach him a thing or two—help him become a man. But now…part of me worries keeping everyone's insides twisted up and worrying over him is all John knows how to do." Hayden sighed. "It's not his fault. He learned all that from Ed."

The mention of their deceased stepfather had John clenching his fists. It'd taken him a while to figure out that his charismatic stepfather was really a master manipulator—*after* Ed had used him to all but empty out the ranch accounts. It was something John had to live with, every day. Hearing Hayden comparing *him* to *Ed* had John seeing red. He wasn't Ed. Dammit all, he wasn't. Hayden had said a lot of things about him, but this was the worst. Is that what Hayden thought? John wanted to hurt people? To manipulate people? His carefully practiced speech went out the window as he stepped into the barn, all but shaking with anger. "Are you saying I'm full of shit? Lazy? Manipulative? Or a thief? Which, exactly, did I learn from our late stepfather? Or is it all of the above?"

"John?" Hayden stared at him, in shock, before a smile creased his face.

"John?" Kyle ran at him, full steam, but John sidestepped his would-be embrace.

He hated that he wobbled and that his brothers both saw it and glanced at his leg. Even more, he hated the rush of sympathy that changed both of their expressions. "Don't let a bum knee throw you off, Hayden. You were in the middle of something good."

Hayden's smile faded, and he ran a hand over his face. "I was spouting off, angry—"

"I always did bring out the best in you. Sounds like nothing's changed." John felt his bravado slipping. "What did I do this time?"

Hayden's gaze locked with his, his brow furrowing.

"Can you two call a cease-fire for a few minutes?" Kyle looked back and forth between them. "It'd be nice to be in the same room as both my brothers for more than five minutes." He gripped John's arm. "Did you see Mom?"

"That's where I came from, why she called." John nodded, tearing his gaze from Hayden's. "To tell you I was home. I thought surprising you was a good idea." He shook his head. *Joke's on me.* "I don't know what I was thinking."

"You staying?" Kyle asked.

From the corner of his eye, John saw Hayden stiffen. Brace, more like it. He swallowed down the lump clogging his throat long enough to say, "No." He shook his head. "Just…passing through. I made some plans." The plan now was to get the hell out of here. *Fast.* He ignored Hayden, his tight-pressed lips and flared nostrils. "But, you know, I'll be back after a while. I won't miss your wedding, Kyle. I'm happy for you." He was, too. He was happy for both of his brothers. He'd planned on saying as much.

"John, wait a minute." Hayden cleared his throat. "Don't go off—"

"'Half-cocked and fuming'?" John filled in, making sure they knew what he'd heard. He didn't want to hurt this way. He'd rather be angry than hurt. He could burn through anger. Being compared to Ed? Knowing his brother believed he was like the man that'd damn near broken their family? It hurt. It hurt a hell of a lot.

"Shit." Kyle ran a hand along the back of his neck.

"It's fine," John reassured them both. "It's like

we're picking up where we left off." He shrugged. "But we'll have to save round two for another time." He didn't wait for more. His knee throbbed when he turned sharply, but he didn't let it slow him down. Knowing Kyle, he'd try to smooth things over and pretend the years-old tension and resentment weren't all that bad. *As if that was possible.* He veered around the house and headed straight for his Jeep where Alpha sat waiting. "You ready?" he asked, climbing up and starting the engine. "Let's go see Nat. She owes me a drink."

Chapter Three

"Can I get a burger with that shake?" Benny, a Bear's House regular, propped himself up on his elbows and gave Nat a wink.

Nat slid a menu across the counter. "Our burgers are on special, Benny. You're in luck." She went back to drying the beer glasses and putting them onto the shelves that lined the wall behind the bar. "There's a table over there, if you like."

"Hells bells, darlin'. I like this view better," Benny said. "I don't care much for them stick-figure types. All poky angles and…and flat. With you, I wouldn't have to worry about that. There's nothing flat about you."

Nat was a proud size twelve. She'd always struggled with her weight. Her feast-or-famine childhood saw her hungry for days. When food was around, she tended to binge until she was sick. It'd been a hard habit to break. But when she'd started school in Granite Falls and some of the little girls chanted *Natty is a fatty* on the playground, she'd tried. Grampa Bear saw her struggle and had given her the advice she lived her life by.

The sooner you get comfortable with yourself and your body, the sooner you'll stop giving credence to what other people say and think. He'd given her a long, steady look. *You should know, Nat, the ones picking and poking fun, those are the folk with something missing inside, not you. You be you, and don't let anyone or anything change that.* Grampa Bear had wiped away her tears and taken her for a motorcycle ride in the sidecar he'd added just for her.

That was it. She would never be a size four, ever, and she was okay with that. She loved cake and ice cream, bread and pasta, and…food.

"Do you want your usual, Benny? With bacon and cheese?" Not that she needed to ask. Benny was here every Tuesday and Thursday, same time, same stool and same food.

"You read my mind, Nat." Benny nodded. "And a shake, too." He winked.

Nat turned in his order, took off her apron and hung it on the hook in the kitchen. She took a few minutes to catch up the night manager, Walt Stewart, before leaving. It was a Thursday night so football fans would be coming in soon; other than that, it should be a relatively quiet evening.

"I'm thinking about taking tomorrow off," Nat said, watching Walt's reaction. She had to do something to get John moving. "You think you and Zeke can handle it?"

"Yup." Walt nodded.

"You're sure?" This was hard. She never, ever took time off.

"Yup." Walt nodded again. "Everythin' okay?"

"Yes." She smoothed her hands over her jeans. "Just…you know, taking a day."

Walt's eyes narrowed. "Okay."

"Okay." She swallowed back any explanation; she had to. John had stayed inside her property line for the last ten days. As far as she knew, no-body outside of the Mitchell family knew that John Mitchell had stepped foot in Granite Falls. John hadn't shared the details of his failed family re-union, only that his family thought he'd left town, and he wanted to keep it that way for now. From the way he'd avoided her gaze to the defiant thrust of his chin, Nat knew he was hurting and relented.

But it had been ten days of no people or ques-tions, and Nat was beginning to worry. Sure, John had done some odd jobs around the house before filling his time with whatever it was he did most hours in Bear's shop, but it wasn't good for him to hide from the rest of the world. "Just call me if you need me." She patted Walt's arm.

"Yup." Walt sighed. "'Night."

"'Night, Walt." She waved. "Thanks." She pushed the front door open and walked out onto the gravel parking lot. Other than Benny's old beat-up truck, the lot was empty.

The Bear's House was on the very edge of town on a stretch of Main Street a few miles before that street became a state highway. Every evening since John had arrived, Nat's ten-minute walk had taken more and more time. Between the Bear's House's financial situation and John's continued descent into this sort of self-imposed exile, she needed the time to think.

The problem was, she was rapidly running out of ideas for how to deal with either situation.

The Bear's House had back taxes to pay. No small amount, either. Grampa Bear hadn't known about it: their accountant had done a good job of making it look like things were on the up-and-up. But he'd supposedly retired a couple of years back and taken the Bear's House tax money. She'd found out he'd done the same thing with several other small businesses he'd been working for, too. Too bad he'd moved to Vanuatu, a nonextradition country, and invested all their money into citizenship there.

Unless she came up with some sort of fundraising idea that Granite Falls would support, she was out of luck. And soon… How could she rally Granite Falls to save the Bear's House when a fair amount of the population would happily see it close? She ran a hand over her hair and smoothed it into place.

She turned off Main Street and walked the eight

blocks toward her home. The house was at the end of Hackberry Lane, a dead-end street. Grampa Bear had been fond of privacy and very low maintenance. Other than mowing the grass and trimming the occasional low-lying or dead tree limb, he hadn't done much to their oversize lot, letting it become a haven for a menagerie of wild creatures and birds.

As she reached the gate, she saw Alpha stand and trot, slowly, toward the gate. One thing she'd learned, everything about Alpha moved in slow motion. Nat loved the old guy and the way he came out to welcome her home.

While Alpha was settling in just fine, Vlad still wasn't too thrilled about the dog's arrival. Being a much larger—and therefore far more threatening—creature, Vlad wasn't sure how to put Alpha in his place. He growled and hissed and ran around the dog, making all sorts of threatening sounds, but Alpha couldn't care less, which infuriated the one-eyed raccoon even more. Not that she and John didn't enjoy Vlad's performances.

"Hey, Alpha," she said, opening the gate and giving him a good rubdown. "Did he go up to the shop?" She glanced at the line of trees that partially hid Grampa Bear's workshop from view. "Did he do anything new today? Or is his leg still bothering him?" Two nights ago, it'd rained and ratcheted up the pain in John's knee and his grumpiness. He'd gone from being withdrawn but productive to grouchy and sedentary.

Alpha's ears perked up, his eyes on her face, but he didn't answer.

"Or call his family? A friend?" Anyone? She followed the senior dog down the path and up the stairs onto the front porch. She took a deep breath and opened the door. "I'm home," she called out.

Nothing.

She gave Alpha a shrug and ventured into the dim house, turning on lights as she went. With the blinds shut, the drapes drawn and the lights off, the gloom was enough to make her feel blue and want to burrow into Grampa Bear's recliner. It was no wonder John was in such a state. Light, sunlight preferably, instantly changed the tomb-like living room into a cheery place to visit and chat…or watch television all day. From the looks of it, that is exactly what John had done. He lay on the couch, his left leg propped up on pillows, the television on and the volume blaring.

"Clint Eastwood again?" The squinty-eyed actor was glaring at her from the television screen. "Did you find a twenty-four-hour Clint Eastwood channel?" And hadn't he already watched this one? But all the Clint Eastwood cowboy movies looked the same to her.

"Ha," John mumbled.

It was a sort of acknowledgment.

"Anything new?" she asked, setting her purse on the kitchen counter. "You and Alpha get into all sorts of trouble?"

"Nah." Another mumble.

Maybe I need to work on my sarcasm? "Knee still hurting?"

"Yeah." He didn't bother looking at her.

She felt for him, she did. Grampa Bear had had terrible arthritis, and there were days every movement caused him pain—especially on rainy days. "Hopefully tomorrow will be better."

He didn't respond this time.

With a sigh, she turned to see the answering-machine light blinking.

"Who called?" she asked, pulling a glass from the kitchen cupboard and the pitcher of iced tea from the refrigerator.

"Dunno." This time, he sounded irritated.

She shot him a look. *Really?* She pressed the button and sipped her tea.

"Hi. This is Emily Walsh. I'm looking for John Mitchell. He gave me this number as his emergency contact." The woman paused and said her phone number. "It's very important that he call me at this number," she added before hanging up.

"Did you hear that?" she asked, writing down the name and phone number.

Nothing.

She moved around the couch and stood in front

of him, blocking his view of the television. "John?" she asked. "The phone message was for you. Did you hear it?"

"I don't know any Emily Walsh." He shrugged, shifting on the couch so he could see the screen.

That made no sense whatsoever. Nat sighed. When he didn't react, she did it again—as loudly as possible.

"What?" he asked, his gaze fixed on the television.

"I guess I'm wondering why a perfect stranger left a message saying you'd given her my number as an emergency contact. A little weird, don't you think?"

He shrugged.

"I think it's weird." She waited for him to say something—anything. Nothing. "Could it be someone from the military?"

"No," he all but growled.

He had the right to rest and recharge, and she wanted that for him, but that didn't stop her from worrying about him. There was a difference between recharging and hiding from everything and everyone. She had never seen him like this. And while she liked having him here and he was, without a doubt, the world's most gorgeous couch potato, it wasn't doing him any good. Getting him up, moving, doing might help shake off this funk. *Hopefully*. She'd start small. "I was hoping you'd give me a hand with dinner?" She pressed her hand to her head. "I have a headache and could use a hand."

John's brown eyes finally looked her way. "You do?"

It went against everything for her to lie but... she managed to nod.

"Sorry." He sat up, clicked off the television and sighed. "What can I do?"

"Chili? Or breakfast for dinner? Some bacon, eggs, biscuits?"

"Breakfast." He stood, taking a minute to steady himself, before moving into the kitchen. "You do the biscuits, I'll do the bacon and eggs?"

"You cook?" she asked, joining him in the galley kitchen.

"Bacon and eggs." The corner of his mouth kicked up.

"What else do you need, right?" She smiled at him.

"Protein with a side of protein." His gaze wandered over her face, lingering on her eyes first—then her lips. "Gotta stay strong." He sounded slightly strained, the slight curve to his mouth going flat.

She'd gotten him up and off the couch. *This is good.* He was talking. *One thing at a time.* "Buttermilk? Corn? Cinnamon? Sour cream?"

"I'm not sure what you're asking." His gaze bounced back up, his brown eyes meeting hers.

"Biscuits." She kept on smiling. "Oh, wait, I have some of my homemade strawberry jam left. Are you okay with buttermilk? They go best with the jam."

"Sure."

"Well, gosh, if you're not interested, I'll save it." She started assembling her ingredients. "It takes blood, sweat and tears to make the stuff, so I don't break it out for just anyone." She paused, giving him a look. "I'm serious."

It wasn't much of a smile. "I'm honored that you're sharing your jam with me."

She made a disapproving sound. "We'll see. I guess it depends on your bacon and eggs." Instead of forcing conversation, she turned to making biscuits. Flour, eggs, buttermilk, she added this and that, knowing the recipe by heart.

Whether or not it was intentional, John was making all sorts of noise, from the bang of the cast-iron skillet on the gas burners to the vigorous sound of the fork hitting and scraping the side of one of her daisy-painted mixing bowls. She winced, hoping he wouldn't break one of her treasured Grampa Bear presents. He proceeded to drop two eggs on the floor, let Alpha clean up the mess and kept right on going. She got out the disinfectant spray and shooed Alpha aside so she could clean and wipe away any egg residue.

He dumped the bowl, fork and eggshells into

the sink before opening the refrigerator and pulling out the bacon. Another skillet, more slamming and the teeth-grinding slide of metal spatula on her no-stick skillet.

Nat glanced his way more than once, her frustration mounting. When the smell of burning bacon reached her, she turned and pushed against his shoulder. "I'll take over, and you can tell me what's wrong."

"Nothing." He leaned against the kitchen counter.

"I call bull. You seem to forget that I *know* you." She pulled the smoking skillet from the too-high burner and set it on the marble countertop, dumped the eggs, dried out and flecked with an excessive amount of black pepper, directly into the trash, and the bacon and eggshells, too. "You're making your Clint Eastwood squinty-eyed glare thing. That means you're mad. You've never lied to me before, John Henry Mitchell." She thumped the pan, hard, against the trash can for emphasis. "Don't you dare start now."

Yes, she knew how to read him, but he knew how to read her. That was one thing that hadn't changed. "How's your head?"

Nat swallowed, her gaze bouncing from the pan to the middle of his chest.

Gotcha. Nat had lied to him. If she hadn't, she

would have been able to make eye contact. Instead, she avoided his gaze *and* visibly paled *and* did that eyebrow-bounce thing that she did when she was hiding something. He knew each tell well. It was exactly how she reacted when they'd been kids and she'd tried to cover up for him when he'd done something wrong. It hadn't worked then, and it wouldn't work now. "You've always been a terrible liar, Nat."

That caught her attention. Those blue eyes flashed when they met his. "Fine. You're right. I don't have a headache."

He nodded. "I know. Why'd you say you did?" As soon as he asked the question, he regretted it. Chances were, he didn't want to hear the answer.

Her lips pressed flat, like she had a lot to say but was holding back. He couldn't decide if that was a good thing or a bad thing.

Suddenly, Nat's eyes narrowed as she took in the state of her kitchen. "Is that why you did *this*? Wasting food? To make me come clean?"

"Maybe." When she put it that way, he sounded like a child.

With a sigh, she set the pan down and glanced at the mixing bowl he'd been using. "I'm no better, I guess. I could have asked for your help…" She swallowed. "I just… I guess…"

"You thought I'd say no?" He ran a hand along the back of his neck.

She nodded, her eyes locking with his. "You've been a little grumpy the last couple of days."

Dammit all. Now he felt like an ass. "You want my help making dinner?" He cleared his throat. Nat deserved to be treated better. He needed to *do* better.

"If you're feeling up to it." She paused, smiling slightly. "And if you *can* actually cook bacon and eggs."

"Oh, I can cook, all right." He grinned. "I'll make you the best bacon and eggs you've ever tasted."

"Those are big words, sir." She offered him the dirty pan.

He eyed it. "How about I wash it first?"

"That would be good." She stepped out of the way of the sink. "I'll get back to making the biscuits. *But* be careful with that bowl. Grampa Bear got it for me."

John winced, feeling like an even bigger ass. If he'd broken it… "I didn't know."

"How could you?" She placed her hand on his arm and gave him a squeeze. "We're just working through the kinks is all."

John felt the tension drain from the room and could breathe easier. Just when he thought he was making progress with his temper, he went and did something like this. He wasn't five; he could have asked Nat what was up instead of slamming around and making things worse. Maybe he wasn't making progress after all. If he wasn't careful, he'd do something stupid, like this, and wind up losing Nat, too.

Not that Nat was holding on to it. Nope. She chattered away about her day, barely pausing for breath. He didn't interrupt; it wasn't like he had anything to add. Besides, he liked watching her talk. It was a full-body experience. From the shift of emotions on her face to the constant motion of her hands, Nat was quite a storyteller.

By the time they'd finished dinner—Nat was right, they were the best damn biscuits he had ever put in his mouth—and his passable bacon and eggs, played a few hands of dominoes and cleaned up the kitchen together, Nat had chatted him into an almost good mood.

"I've got tomorrow off." Nat yawned. "Got some stuff to do around here. Maybe you could help me?" She shrugged. "I'm too tired to think right now. 'Night." With another yawn, she disappeared down the hall, the click of her bedroom door echoing in the quiet.

It was quiet, too quiet, so he went back to the movie marathon and her comfy couch. But one and a half Clint Eastwood movies later, he was hungry again.

Biscuits. There'd been a good half dozen left. Add some of her homemade jam, and he had himself the perfect midnight snack. "Sounds good to me." He winked at Alpha, pushed off the couch and headed into the kitchen. He warmed three biscuits in the microwave, pulled the butter and jam from the fridge and carried it all to the table.

He reached for the crossword puzzle Nat had left for him and knocked the pile of letters and mail beside the paper onto the floor. *Great.* He bent forward, stooping to collect the papers while Alpha used his nose to push envelopes closer. "Thanks, old man."

Alpha's tail wagged in answer.

A white envelope caught his eye. A white envelope with the words Immediate Action Required. From the IRS. The paper was tucked half in and half out... Enough for him to read a few alarming words. Words like *past due* and *back taxes* and *forfeit property.* He laid the envelope on the table, seriously considering reading the entirety of the letter.

He swallowed the biscuit he was chewing, but it stuck in his throat. Was this for the house? Or the Bear's House? Either way, it was worrisome. And Nat was dealing with it—on her own. Why hadn't she told him? *Probably for the same reason she didn't ask for my help.* He'd been grumpy, as she put it, and pretty damn useless so far, so why tell him?

Out of the corner of his eye, he saw movement. Nat. He watched her, barefoot and wearing a threadbare pink and white robe, tiptoe across the kitchen. She headed to the kitchen cabinet, opened the door and rifled around.

She pulled out a bottle of pain relievers and a glass. She took three, not two, and set the bottle on the counter, then swallowed down the pills with some water.

He frowned. "How's the head?" he asked.

She jumped, knocking the pill bottle onto the floor. "Dagnabbit, John, you scared me half to death." She pressed a hand to her chest before stooping for the bottle. "Glad the lid was on." She stood, pressing her fingers to her temples and glanced at his plate. "You liked those biscuits, didn't you?"

"Yes, ma'am, I did. Delicious." He held up his last biscuit, topped with a healthy dollop of jam. "This jam is like heaven in a jar, too."

"It was my best batch yet." Nat's smile was small and tired and…*sad.*

John didn't like feeling helpless, but he didn't know what to do. Bear had always seemed pretty business savvy, so this was a surprise. Unless this had started after Bear had died? Was she having a hard time managing the Bear's House on her own? Was she embarrassed that she'd let this happen? Did she think he'd judge her or blame her? She knew better than that. Sure, it might not be something she wanted to talk about—he understood that all too well—but this wasn't about some harsh words exchanged years ago. This was about losing her home or the Bear's House. He was pretty sure the IRS wasn't going to let her off the hook or go away. "Nat, you okay?"

Nat sighed and turned, her blue eyes meeting his.

Dammit all. She'd been crying. *Not so okay, then.* Her eyes were red-rimmed; her nose was red-tipped, too.

She stared at him for a long time before she said, "Just a headache. A real one. I'll be fine once those pain relievers kick in. And I get some sleep." He didn't buy a word of it. "But do you mind putting that in the dishwasher when you're through and running it?" she asked, nodding at his almost empty plate. "I would appreciate it."

"Sure." Whatever she needed.

"Thanks." Her smile was wobbly and pathetic. "I'm going to bed. See you in the morning." She rinsed out her cup and set it aside before heading for the door.

Nat was the strongest, most independent person he knew. The most resilient, too. But some things were too big to handle alone. The tears in her eyes said as much. He knew he was a useless, selfish piece of shit, but he wasn't blind. This was eating Nat up. He couldn't stand it. He didn't know what or if there was anything he could do, but what sort of person—sort of friend—was he if he didn't try? *Say something.* He sucked in a deep breath. "Nat?" He turned to find her standing in the doorway.

She waited, her hand resting on the door frame, an almost hopeful expression on her face. She did that, looked at him like he was somebody special. Once upon a time, that look had put him on top of the world. Now? It was too much for him. Over the last couple of years, John had come to terms with that fact, that he was a disappointment, a screwup. He'd heard it almost daily from his superior officers—and his big brother before that. He didn't want to make a bad situation worse by getting involved. He'd only let her down. It was better that she didn't get her hopes up over him. Or have any expectations, either. She might not have given up on him, but it didn't matter. He'd given up on himself when he was pulled from the rubble that destroyed his leg, his career and his future. He rubbed his knee. "'Night." He cleared his throat. "I hope you get some sleep and feel better."

"Me, too." She nodded. Those blue eyes never left his face, but there was no hint of disappointment or anger or judgment there. Nat always gave him the benefit of the doubt. *Even when she shouldn't.* "'Night, John. Sweet dreams." With a small smile, she waved and disappeared into the darkness of the hall.

I'm a cowardly son of a bitch. He didn't want to make her sad. He didn't want to disappoint her. But he didn't know what to do…about anything. Chances were, she'd picked up on what a mess he was. If he came right out and told her how lost he felt, he couldn't take that back. She had enough to worry about.

He slumped in his chair, fed the last of the biscuit to Alpha, loaded his dishes into the dishwasher and turned it on. It wasn't his business, and there wasn't a thing he could do about it, but he reached for the IRS letter and read it front to back, anyway.

"Shit. This is bad." He glanced at Alpha. "*Bad* bad."

Alpha cocked his head to one side.

He scanned the letter again. "Five years?" Back taxes accrued over a five-year period, long before Bear had died. How did something like that happen? That didn't sound like Bear. He sure as hell wouldn't have left her with this sort of burden, that much was certain.

Nat had been everything to Bear. When she came to Granite Falls, he'd changed. He'd fitted his prize Harley-Davidson motorcycle with a sidecar and, almost overnight, gone from being the scary biker guy that yelled at people to the man who showed up to help out at every festival and event. If there was a way to get Nat involved and connected with the community, Bear made sure she was there. He wanted to make up for all the horrible things Nat had dealt with before coming here, things John knew little about. So, this—leaving this sort of mess—didn't add up.

Not only could she lose the Bear's House, there was a chance they could take the house, too. Nat could lose everything. He scanned the letter a final time and tucked it back into the envelope.

"She's in a world of hurt, Alpha." He rubbed the big dog's head. "Damn, but life isn't fair." He didn't need more proof of that; he was reminded every damn day.

As much as he'd like to blame his commanding officer, Lieutenant Dan Rogers, for what had happened to him, he knew better. It was his own damn fault, all of it. A sort of cosmic justice for all the shit he'd pulled and, somehow, managed to get away with. Not that Lt. Rogers hadn't been an ass: the man's picture was probably in the dictionary right beside the word. He and John had shared one thing—a mutual dislike for one another. But Lt. Rogers was his superior, and he loved to lord that fact over John, always looking for ways to get him riled up or acting up. Invariably, John did just that. The latest? A Willful Dereliction in Performance of Duties charge. He'd been waiting to hear his punishment in the discipline barracks when a wave of drones had stuck, raining grenades and causing all sorts of chaos. He'd been alone, buried beneath what was left of the disciplinary barracks, for hours while the damage to the rest of the base was assessed. As far as the rest of the base knew, those barracks were empty, and in all the fallout, Lt. Rogers had forgotten John was there.

At first, John hadn't wanted to believe he'd been forgotten. His lieutenant had never bothered to hide what he thought of John. Maybe the man figured John was getting what he deserved. But once John's anger had faded and he'd seen the devastation the attack had caused, he accepted that Lt. Rogers had done his job. John wasn't the only man wounded that day. He was lucky to still be alive. It had been a wake-up call. An eye-opening, self-loathing-inducing moment that had Hayden's words cycling through his head, over and over.

The world doesn't revolve around you. He could hear Hayden's parting speech like it was yesterday. *You're going to be part of a team, John, and your team and superiors will expect you to do your part. Lives may very well depend on you doing just that. Sure, you can push back, alienate your team, make enemies and get pissed off, but you won't last long in the service. I hope you're listening, even if it is all coming from me. It's time for you to grow up, John. I hope like hell you'll get a grip on your temper and step up before you get someone killed.*

He sighed, rubbing Alpha behind the ear. Now that he knew *he* was responsible, thinking about

Lt. Rogers, his team, the bombing, the hours of lying there—scared and bleeding, that left him with permanent damage—wasn't easy. He had made the choices that led up to that fateful day.

Nat had not. "If anyone deserves a break, it's Nat," John said, giving Alpha a belly rub. Then again… *Life isn't fair.*

Chapter Four

Nat pushed her cart down the chip aisle, loading up John's preferred super-hot corn chips that Nat couldn't stand the smell of, let alone imagine tasting. More of his smokehouse almonds, too. She turned into the next aisle, slid a large bag of Alpha's dog food onto the bottom of the cart and headed for some produce, then beer. It was when she was reaching for the apples that she spied Jan Mitchell, John's mother.

No. No, no, no. She forgot about the apples and hurried from the produce. It was one thing to keep it quiet so the world didn't know John had been at her place for almost three weeks now. It was a whole other thing to look his *mother* in the eye and not immediately confess John had been hiding at her place. And that is exactly what he was doing. Hiding. Yes, he'd been pulling his own weight—and then some—around the house, but he still hadn't ventured beyond her property line or shared what he was struggling with. Whatever it was, she knew his family would be there for him. Especially his mother. Jan Mitchell was a good mother. She loved her sons. She was proud of her sons.

She'd be devastated if she knew John has been here all this time.

After putting a twelve-pack of longneck beer into her cart, Nat headed toward the front of the store, eager to check out and leave. She pushed her cart up and began unloading her groceries onto the checkout counter.

"You okay, sugar?" Wilma Smith asked, scanning each item—one by one—at a glacial pace. "You seem awful jumpy."

"I'm good, thanks, Wilma." Nat smiled. "How are you?"

Wilma raised one painted-on eyebrow. "I've been ringing up your groceries for years, and I've never seen you buyin' this much alcohol."

Nat eyed the twelve-pack.

"And dog food?" Wilma gave her an odd look. "When did you get a dog?"

"It's for the raccoon…" She laughed, nervous.

"Is the beer for the raccoon, too?" Wilma asked, her bright red lips smiling. "You be careful of those things. Raccoons, I mean. They carry all sorts of disease. Rabies, too. You shouldn't feed 'em."

Nat nodded. "I'll keep that in mind."

"You should. My sister, Irma-Lou, she got bit right on the finger by a skunk, and she ended up getting a nasty infection. Blood poisoning." Wilma kept talking as she worked.

Nat didn't know how a skunk bite had anything to do with a raccoon, but she didn't interrupt. Vlad was a curmudgeon, but she had a hard time imagining him biting her. Still, Nat didn't share her thoughts or interrupt Wilma. If Wilma was in the midst of the story, she wouldn't ask Nat questions. The less questions, the better.

"Natalie?" Jan Mitchell.

Of course. Nat turned, her heart thudding against her rib cage. "Hi, Mrs. Mitchell."

"Natalie Harris, you know to call me Jan." Jan held her by the shoulders. "I haven't seen you in so long. How are you? Are you taking care of yourself?"

Nat nodded. *I'm taking care of myself. And John.* She swallowed, her heart faster now.

"You look good." Jan smiled. "Why don't you come out to the house for dinner sometime soon?" Every time she and Jan had crossed paths, Jan would ask her to dinner.

"I'd like that." Which was the same answer she always gave Jan. It sounded like she was agreeing— when she was really dodging. Normally, it was because Nat's hours were erratic and it was easier not to go. *This time I* can't *come because I'm keeping a secret from you.* Nat felt ill.

"You haven't seen the kids in a while. Mya is

doing so well with her cochlear implant. And little Weston is talking a mile a minute. They grow so fast. Too fast." Jan's adoration for her children and grandchildren was unabashed.

"I'm so glad. I know it was a big operation." Except for John, the Mitchell family seemed to be entering a new phase. Kids, marriages, being happy... Nat glanced at the checkout counter. Wilma was still sliding things through, looking more than perturbed by Jan's interruption.

"Mya is a marvel. They all are. Not that I'm biased, of course." Jan smiled. "I hope you'll come for Kyle and Skylar's wedding. It would mean a lot. It would be the next best thing to having John there—considering how close you two always were."

Nat swallowed, suddenly hot. *Speaking of which, he's at my place...dealing with something. Not that he'll tell me what...* He'd rather change light bulbs, replace a line of pipe in the sprinkler system and give all of Grampa Bear's motorcycles a tune-up than talk about what was eating him up inside.

"Are you all right, Nat?" Jan asked.

"I asked her the same thing," Wilma piped up. "She's been drinking too much beer and eating too many of those chips. They'll eat your intestinal lining, don't you know? It's no wonder she's a little piqued."

Nat wished the floor would open up, right then

and there. "I'm fine," she assured them both. "Tired. That's all." *And I'm a liar.*

Jan didn't look convinced, and from the way she inventoried Nat's groceries, it was clear the woman was concerned.

Thanks a lot, Wilma.

"Really." Nat went on, "I've been working extra hours at the Bear's House—"

"Hmph," Wilma mumbled. She wasn't a fan because her brother, Benny, spent far too much time there.

Nat pretended the woman hadn't spoken. "I guess the extra hours are showing." *And all the lying and pressure about money and hiding John isn't helping, either.* She watched Wilma slide the last can of tuna over the scanner and breathed a sigh of relief. "I'm headed home now."

"You promise me you'll take a nap?" Jan asked. "Maybe see about taking a day or two off, too. I know Bear would be proud of you, working as hard as you do, but he'd never want you to put your health in jeopardy."

Grampa Bear. She swallowed. *He'd definitely be disappointed in me for lying.* Nat nodded, watching the bagger finish packing up all her items into the reusable shopping bags she'd brought with her. "I will get some rest."

"And maybe cut back a little," Wilma said, pointing at the beer. "That's not an easy-to-break habit."

Nat nodded again. "Will do, Wilma. I hope your sister's finger is okay now."

Wilma nodded. "The part they saved is just fine." She waited for Nat to pay, then handed over her receipt. "See you next week."

"It was nice seeing you, Nat." Jan hugged her, whispering, "If there's ever anything I can do for you—even if it's just to sit and listen—I'd be happy to do it."

Nat pressed her eyes shut and hugged the woman back. *Your son has been living at my place for three weeks, and I'm so worried about him. He's lost his smile, Jan. And I might be losing my home and Grampa Bear's business. But, other than that, I'm fine.* "I appreciate that." She let go of the woman, waved and pushed her cart out of the store as quickly as possible.

She loaded up the bed of Bear's ancient, beat-up truck and climbed in the cab, taking the long way home to buy her some alone time. Like it or not, she and John had to talk. Tonight. Her nerves were stretched taut without having to lie to a woman she considered family. She and John were close, but they were both still keeping secrets from one another. No more. By the time she pulled into the driveway, she was determined. No more beating around the bush or changing the subject or escaping for some urgent odd job he'd discovered. Tonight, they were talking. Period. She took a deep breath and turned off her truck. But her heart slammed to a stop when she spied a strange blue sedan parked in front of the house, with the engine running.

Was it the IRS? Did they come to your home? Was she going to be questioned? How did this work? *Calm down, Nat. Calm.* She'd called one of Bear's retired lawyer friends, Cliff Nichols, who said he'd look into things. He *had* said they wouldn't just kick her out. *I'm going to hold you to that, Mr. Nichols.*

She climbed out of the truck and moved to its rear, pulling out the shopping bags and heading toward the front door, not sparing a glance at the car.

"Hello?" a woman called out.

Nat took a deep breath and turned. "Yes?"

"I'm looking for John Mitchell?" The woman shaded her eyes. "My name is Emily Walsh. I've left a few messages? John had given me your information—in case of emergency."

Not the IRS. Nat breathed a little easier. And yet… Why was Emily Walsh here? Why did she have Nat's information as John's emergency contact? Why would she need John's emergency contact information when John swore he didn't know an Emily Walsh?

"Oh, hello." Nat set the bags on the front porch and walked down the path to the gate. "What can I do for you, Miss Walsh?"

"I'm looking for John. Right away. It *is* an emergency." She shook her head. "I know he is here. I saw his dog, Alpha, through the window." She leveled a cold stare Natalie's way. "I'd rather we didn't pretend he wasn't."

"Okay." Nat sighed. *Come on, John.* This was the last thing she needed. Whatever Emily Walsh wanted, John should be the one dealing with it. Not her.

"I don't know if he's avoiding me or if he hasn't received my messages, but there is *something* he needs to know about…" Her voice rose.

Nat couldn't decide whether to be offended or not. John only knew about the messages because Nat had played them—loudly. Why would she try to keep them from John?

"So can I talk to him?" Emily pointed at the house. "I've been banging on the door and calling, and he isn't answering."

"He might be in the shop out back." If he wasn't answering, there had to be a reason. Still, Nat didn't want to get in the middle of this. Whatever this was.

"He's here. That's all I care about." Emily Walsh came around the car and pulled open the back door, talking the whole time. "I can't do this. I can't. I'm giving her up for adoption if he doesn't want her—the paperwork is signed and ready to go. But he'd gone on and on and on about his family, so I figured I'd ask him first." She pulled an infant car seat out of the back seat and set it on the sidewalk. "He can get her DNA tested if he thinks I'm lying. She is his."

All Nat could do was stare at the teeny-tiny sleeping pink bundle.

"She's almost a month old," Emily Walsh said. "I tried. I really tried," the woman sobbed. "But I never thought one weekend with some random, wounded, hot soldier would lead to…her. I'm a dancer. We'd just docked and only had two nights in Fort Lauderdale before the next cruise, so I thought, why not live a little? We had a good time, went our separate ways and then…this happened… I can't keep her." She barely glanced at the infant. "I'm a terrible person."

That snapped Nat out of it. "No, you're not." She shook her head. "If you *know* you can't be a mother, then you're trying to do what's best for…"

"Leslie," Emily said, sniffing. "I am. I really am."

"That's not a terrible thing, Emily. That's a good thing." Nat's heart hurt for the woman. "Leslie will come to appreciate your decision." It wouldn't be easy, but it was so much better than living with someone who didn't want you. "And I'm sure John's family will want to know about her." Jan would be devastated to learn she had a granddaughter she might never have known.

"You think so?" Emily's tears wouldn't stop, even as she continued to unload bags and boxes onto the sidewalk. "You don't think she'll hate me when she grows up?" She eyed the car seat. "I don't want her to hate me."

"I know so." Nat couldn't remember all the times her mother had told Nat she should have given her up for adoption. Over and over. She'd hated Nat. She'd blamed Nat for everything that went wrong. And for years, Nat had believed her. This was different. This was a woman doing the right thing for her child.

"Good. You're Nat, right?"

"Yes." Nat nodded.

"He said you were the best. I can see why he said that. I feel a whole lot better about this now. And meeting you, too." Emily wiped her tears away and nodded. "That's all of her stuff."

About this... That's is all of her stuff... That's when Nat realized what was happening. "Wait—"

"John." Emily nodded, looking over Nat's shoulder.

Thank goodness. Yes, John, come deal with this. Nat turned, but there was no one on the porch, no John to witness the arrival of his daughter, no shock and horror and panic. The slam of the car door had Nat spinning back around. "Wait." She knocked on the car window. "Emily, please, wait."

Emily ignored her, turned the car and drove down the street.

"Wait," Nat called out again, her heart in her

throat. "You can't just leave her." But Emily was gone, and there was no one to hear her words. No one but Leslie, who was now wide awake and screaming at the top of her lungs.

Nat stared down at the baby. "I know exactly how you feel, Leslie." She took a deep breath, scooped up the car seat and headed for the front door. "Let's go meet your daddy, little thing. We will get this all straightened out." How, Nat didn't know. But that teeny-tiny squished-up face needed reassuring before it got any redder. Hell, Nat needed reassuring. "It's okay." *No, it isn't.*

Emily had left her phone number—Nat had written it down. She'd give the number to John, he'd call, they'd talk like rational adults and they'd come up with a plan. *They.* Not her. She had no experience with babies… Especially one that wasn't even a month old.

Nat stared down at the baby. John had been home long enough to make a baby but he'd only been here for the last three weeks. What had he been doing all this time? Would any more babies show up? But her joke wasn't funny. "No more letting John Henry Mitchell off the hook. That's *Daddy*, to you." John. A father? She peered down at the blotchy-face, screaming infant. "You ready?"

John was drying off his just-washed hands when he heard the front door slam. "Did you get the beer?" He ran a hand over his face and yawned. "I think I fixed that faucet—"

But the horrible, high-pitched squeaks and squeals drowned out his words.

Was Nat okay?

Had Vlad finally gone rabid? And broken into the house?

Was there some malfunctioning air-raid siren he didn't know about?

What the hell is happening?

Alpha whimpered and shoved his head under the couch, climbing as far underneath as possible.

"Make room for me," John said, wincing as the noise got louder.

Nat appeared, stony-faced and pale, holding the handle of a baby seat with both hands.

"What the hell is that?" he asked, beyond confused.

Nat said something about a delivery. She held out the car seat. "Emily Walsh left this for you." She stared at him.

John glanced at the wailing creature. "What? I didn't hear all of that."

"Emily Walsh," she repeated as she stepped closer, pressing the screaming bundle into his chest. "This is yours."

He blinked, all the blood in his body going cold. "What did you say?" He frowned. "That's not funny."

"No?" Nat asked. "Leslie and I don't think it's one bit funny, either. Oh, this is Leslie." She glanced at the contorted, beet-red baby. "*This* is Leslie. Your daughter."

John took two steps back. "Nope."

Nat sighed. "John—"

"That's not mine." He shook his head, holding up his hands.

"John—"

"No, Nat, I mean it. I don't know what the hell is going on, here." He couldn't breathe, couldn't think. "But *that*…is not mine."

Nat set the car seat on the table, unbuckled the straps and lifted the shrieking banshee out.

Instant silence.

Nat stared at him, stunned. He stared right back, braced and ready for the torture to resume.

"I need you to think, really hard," Nat said, holding the baby like a bomb about to detonate. "Emily. Blonde. Pretty. Tall. Fort Lauderdale. Dancer on a cruise ship?"

Fort Lauderdale? His palms were sweaty. He'd been stateside three days. The sudden surge in his heartbeat couldn't be healthy. The blonde… He remembered. *Damn it all to hell!.* All the air exited his lungs, and he collapsed inwardly. John sat hard on the arm of the couch. Searing pain shot around his knee, down his calf and up his thigh, forcing him to extend his leg.

"Did you hear me?" Nat asked, glancing between him and the baby.

He nodded.

"So…is she your daughter?" Nat sounded… disappointed.

He was feeling pretty disappointed in himself right about now. Could it be his? "I don't know. How could I know?"

"Well, you either slept with Emily Walsh or you didn't." She cradled the baby against her chest, wrapping her arms around it.

It was so damn small. Was that normal? Should they be that small? Which made him ask, "How old is it?"

"*She* is almost a month old," Nat said, her voice pitched low.

He ran a hand over his face. Was that right? How the hell was he supposed to know? Time hadn't held much relevance since he'd been back. "Where is Emily?"

"She left," Nat said, watching him. "She's going to give Leslie up for adoption."

"Oh." John nodded. That made sense. "Okay."

"*Okay?*" Nat asked. "John—"

"Nat, look at me. *Look* at me." He stood, ignoring the pain the sudden movement caused. "I can barely take care of myself. You think I can take care of…of that?" He frowned. "When is she coming back?"

"She didn't say." Nat wasn't looking at him now, she was looking at the baby. "You can either get the groceries or take care of Leslie while I do it. I can't do both. The cold stuff won't keep in this heat."

"I'll go." He shook his head. "I'd just... I'd break it."

"*She* is not an *it*. *She* is a *her*," Nat corrected, without anger. "Fine. Go." She turned, reaching for an envelope that was tucked along the padding of the car seat.

He went, too eager to get away to care about any discomfort his pace was causing. But once he was outside, on the front porch, he leaned against the railing. This was a mistake. It had to be. There had been a lot of drinking involved the first few months he'd been stateside but... He wasn't that careless.

Inside the house, the wailing returned.

Alpha came trotting to the front door, pushing against the screen until he'd opened it wide enough to slip out.

"I know." John patted the dog. "I know." He spied the box and bags on the sidewalk, as well as the groceries poking out of the truck bed. He'd rather work in the heat, carrying stuff and stressing out his knee than deal with it.

Her. Leslie.

Somehow, he managed to get everything inside. But once that was done, he was scared to death Nat would try to hand over the way-too-small, squalling infant. He didn't know the first thing about babies. He did know he was not made to handle something that small. Or breakable. Or loud.

Without comment he put the groceries away and stacked the boxes against the wall in Nat's rarely used formal dining room, doing his best not to draw attention his way. It was only when the bags were empty and the kitchen was neat and tidy that he realized it was quiet. After all the ear-piercing wailing, it was almost too quiet.

He and Alpha exchanged a look.

Alpha whimpered, his tail wagged and he trotted back into the open kitchen and living room that had been their central command for the last however long he'd been here.

John followed reluctantly, peering around the corner to prepare himself.

But he wasn't prepared.

Nat sat in Bear's big rocking recliner, a bottle in one hand, that tiny, breakable baby cradled close, while she hummed what sounded an awful lot like a Van Halen song—she swore eighties rock music was best. He didn't know whether to feel relieved or terrified. Maybe both? No maybe about it. This little thing had appeared out of thin air, and now he was more lost than ever.

First things first, he had to talk to Emily. "What's her number?" John asked.

"Emily?" Nat didn't look at him.

"Yes, Emily." He sighed.

"It's on the counter, by the answering machine." She went back to humming, calm.

He grabbed the paper with Emily's number, dialed and held his breath. They'd talk, figure this out. It would be okay. He waited, listening to it ring. And ring. And ring.

And then her voice mail picked up. "You've reached Emily Walsh's voice mail. You know what to do." Then a long beep.

"Emily." He paused. What the hell was he supposed to say? "I... I'm sorry I missed you today."

Nat glanced at him then. Was she laughing? What was funny about this? Nothing. That's what.

"We need to talk. You need to call me." He swallowed, adding, "She...she can't stay here." He cleared his throat. "I can't take care of her." Understatement of the century. "I don't know where to start. You need to come get her. Right away." He hung up.

Nat shook her head and went back to humming, staring down at the baby.

"Nat." He frowned. "I... I'm sorry about all this." Was this really happening?

"You didn't know." She glanced at him. "Did you?"

He frowned again. "No. No, I did not." He was a

rat bastard but he wouldn't have run out on Emily. He'd freak out, sure… Like he was now.

"What's the plan now?" Nat's question was soft.

Plan? What plan? He was reeling. But then he figured it out. "Do you…want me to leave?" He cleared his throat. If she kicked him out, what choice did he have? Going home? Now? With a baby? He'd swallow his pride… No, dammit, he couldn't. "I'll go, Nat, I will. But I'd appreciate it if you'd give me time for Emily to come and get Leslie first. Then I'll go." He took a deep breath. "You know how Hayden is. What he thinks. I've made peace with the fact that I'll always be a disappointment to him, but this…on top of everything…" He ran his hands over his face, feeling like the failure he was. "Please."

"Fine," she said, not looking at him.

He paused, waiting for more—for something. The longer she stayed silent, the tenser he became. "And?"

"No *and*." She sighed. "I get that you're hurting and working through things, I do. I haven't pushed. But *this* isn't about you, John. She is a living, breathing human. She needs care and peace and quiet and love, and since you can't give it to her, I will. Until Emily gets back." She looked at him. "But she better get here soon, John. I have a job and responsibilities and things I can't put off."

Like the IRS.

"I know. I'll get her back here." He swallowed, so relieved he could barely contain himself. "And you and Vlad will have your house back to yourselves," he tried to tease.

Nat didn't smile. Instead of those blue-blue eyes being full of laughter, they were full of…sadness. He'd done this. All of this. He'd broken his family, blown himself up, got kicked out of the military, dumped it all on Nat and…and this. Leslie? He couldn't wrap his mind around any of this. Him? A father? He shook his head, beyond frustrated. For the first time in his life—intentional or not— he'd fully committed to something: being a complete and total screwup.

But this time, it might have cost him his friendship with Nat. That he regretted. She was all he had left. Maybe, when this was over and it was back to being the two of them again, he could figure out a way to make things right. He didn't want to lose Nat. Whatever he needed to do to prove that to her, he'd do… Well, he'd try.

Chapter Five

Natalie flipped the page on the baby-care book she'd ordered online and had expedited overnight. She and Leslie and John had made it through one night, but none of them could keep going at this rate. Nat had never dealt with a baby before—ever. And as much as she'd love to think the whole natural maternal instinct was a thing, there were practical items that she'd never considered or known that babies needed for their care. Last night had been a lot of trial and error.

But now she knew how much formula Leslie should be getting in each bottle and how often she should be getting a bottle. Thanks to the book, she knew swaddling could comfort a baby and how, exactly, to swaddle. There were handy diaper-changing tips, something Nat was still struggling with, as well as how often to change them. And there were suggestions on burping the baby—something Leslie refused to do. She'd fuss and squirm and scream and wail until Nat feared she'd inflated herself to the point of popping, then burp—startling them both—and instantly fall asleep. It was nerve-racking.

Everything about the last twenty-four hours—and little Leslie—has been nerve-racking.

So far, the color-coded charts and graphs and pointers had given Nat the hope that, when Leslie woke up, things would be a little less terrifying…

Unfortunately, Nat had yet to find *How to stop jumping at every little sound they make while they sleep* listed on the FAQ page. That would have been extremely helpful.

Nat had been panicking over where Leslie could sleep when she remembered a fundraiser the town had done years ago for the county women's shelter. They'd ordered baby boxes—a bassinet or boxinet or something cutesy like that—that came with all sorts of essential baby supplies. The box itself was sturdy enough to be used as a bassinet and took up far less space than a crib or bassinet and cost next to nothing. She'd gone into Bear's office, found an unused banker's box, lined it with a folded quilt and hoped it would suffice for the night. It looked a little bleak—it *was* a box—but she knew it wouldn't be safe to hold Leslie and try to sleep herself. Not that she got that much sleep.

As tired as she was, she couldn't *sleep*. Who knew how long she'd have before Leslie woke and started wailing? Nat had to read, as fast as she could, to be better prepared.

John was listing across the couch, his mouth open and his head back, snoring loudly.

If she wasn't so angry with him, she might find him adorable. But...she was. He'd hovered most of the night. He'd yet to touch Leslie, let alone hold her, but he'd been sort of helpful. He'd read passages from the book, made bottles, and handed over diapers and wipes without being asked. She appreciated it, she did, but she wished he didn't act like she should know all of this already. As if she had any more baby experience than he did.

Coffee. Coffee would help. *Please, let coffee help.*

She stretched, peered into the box where Leslie slept—all properly swaddled since her last diaper change—and tiptoed into the kitchen. Every little sound seemed magnified. As she filled up the coffeepot and scooped the grounds into the paper liner, she winced and paused, hoping her each and every movement didn't rouse the baby.

When she pressed the On button, she relaxed somewhat, stepping back...and onto Alpha's paw. Alpha whimpered, Nat jumped—and slammed her knee into the cupboard, knocking the container of coffee onto the floor. Fine-ground dark-roast coffee rained down all over her tile floor.

"I'm so sorry," she whispered, crouching by Alpha. "I didn't see you."

Alpha gave her hand a lick, then sneezed, a fine dusting of coffee rising in the air.

"Oh, no. Goodness." She sighed, hugging the large dog. "Thank you, Alpha. Here's hoping today is a better day. Right?" She cradled the dog's large head, rubbing his ears and watching as his eyes closed and he leaned in to her touch. "We can do this."

Alpha sneezed again.

"Everything okay?" John asked, rubbing his eyes with the back of his hand.

Nat glared up at him.

"What?" He frowned, blinking several times, his gaze adjusting and traveling over the fine layer of black-brown dust covering most of the kitchen floor, part of the counter, Nat's feet and Alpha. His eyebrows rose as he asked, "Coffee get away from you?"

Alpha sneezed three times in a row.

Nat shook her head, but laughter bubbled up, anyway. She pressed a hand to her mouth, muffling the sound somewhat.

John smiled, a real, honest-to-goodness smile. The sort of smile that made Nat almost forget his behavior the last few weeks. Almost. But not quite.

She stood. "Alpha wanted to help."

"You did this?" he asked the dog—whose tail wagged slowly in answer. "Well, you better sweep it up." Alpha's tail kept wagging. "No?"

Nat patted the dog on the head. "I think Alpha's lack of opposable thumbs might hinder the effectiveness of his sweeping abilities. And I'm pretty sure we don't want him licking all of this up. It could make him sick or make his heart rate pick up." She wasn't sure how coffee affected dogs, but she was pretty sure this much coffee was bad for any living thing. She ran her fingers through her hair, tucking the longer strands behind her ear, and glanced John's way. "Can you take him outside while I clean this up?"

John was studying her. "Do you have motorcycles all over your pajamas?"

Nat stared down at her pink pajamas. "Yes. Bear got them for me." And she loved them.

"You ever ride, anymore?" he asked. "You still have Bear's bikes, and they're all in good shape."

"Of course they are. Grampa Bear would have a fit otherwise." She shrugged. "But I don't ride. My heart's not in it." Originally, she'd been planning on donating five of the seven bikes to an at-risk mechanics program Bear had volunteered with. But now… Well, she might have to sell all seven of them to keep her home. The thought tore at her heart. It was as if the remaining bits and pieces of Bear were being taken from her, one by one. That lack of control was defeating. She shrugged again. "I haven't gone riding in a while." She had so much on her mind, all the time.

"Maybe you should." He seemed to be studying her. "Take a break."

Leslie began to make the grunt-fuss sound that instantly drew both Nat's and John's attention.

"Okay." Nat nodded. "I'll get dressed and go." She waited, knowing full well she was about to send him into a panic.

"What?" John's brown eyes were round as saucers. "Nat... I mean... Now?" He glanced at the box. "I just... I..."

"Need my help?" she finished for him. "You need my help with your daughter."

His jaw locked but he nodded. "I need your help."

"Okay." She brushed past him. "Come on, Alpha. Go outside and let Vlad yell at you while your daddy cleans up the coffee and I take care of little Miss Leslie." She opened the back door, smiling as Alpha trotted outside, looking up and around him as if he understood exactly what she was saying and was waiting for Vlad's imminent arrival. "Have fun."

"Where's the broom?" John asked, his gaze returning to the box—where the grunts and squeals and fusses were building.

"In the pantry." Nat crossed to the box. "Hi, little one." She reached inside, scooping up the baby and patting her little back. "I bet you're getting hungry, aren't you? Well, I bet your daddy will make up some formula while we change your diaper, if you like."

Leslie wriggled in her swaddling.

"I know, you're excited." She kept patting the baby's back. "Did you get some sleep?" she asked.

Since Bear's passing, Nat had taken to talking to Vlad for companionship. Leslie wasn't a one-eyed raccoon with a bad attitude, but Nat wanted to make friends with the tiny person wrapped in a blanket. Talking, even a one-sided stream of consciousness, was the only thing Nat had come up with so far.

She kept patting, doing her best to balance Leslie while assembling the things she'd need to make Leslie's bottle.

John stopped sweeping. "What's next?"

"I'll walk you through it." She nodded at him, noting how he backed away when she turned in his direction—as if she was suddenly going to foist the baby on him. It was sort of hysterical. But that might have had more to do with her sleep-deprived state than anything. "Wash your hands first, though. With all that coffee floating around, we don't want her to get sick."

John did as she said, dried his hands on one of her dish towels and picked up the formula jar. He followed the directions, shook up the bottle and handed it over. "Done."

"Thank you." Nat smiled. "Now put some warm

water in that mug for me, so we can warm up the formula."

He frowned. "No microwave?"

"According to the baby book, that is a big no-no. The chance of it heating unevenly and then burning her little mouth—"

"Filling the mug." He eyed Leslie while he was warming the tap water. Once he deemed it the right temperature, he filled the mug, put the bottle into the water and stepped back. "Won't she…get upset before it's warm?"

"Yes, there is a high likelihood she will get a tad vocal before the bottle is heated up." Nat bit back a laugh at the renewed panic on John's face.

"Shouldn't we have a bottle ready to go?" he asked. "So, you know, she won't lose it?"

"I guess." Nat kept patting, trying her best not to get irritated. "But formula shouldn't sit around, and since she doesn't have a schedule, there's no way of knowing when to have one ready."

He didn't like that answer, at all. "There has to be a more efficient way to do this."

Nat shrugged. "I'm pretty sure that's what every parent, everywhere, has said when they have a newborn." She nodded at the thick book she'd been perusing. "Feel free to read it. Other than looking up the stuff we needed to know last night, I've gotten through the first few chapters, so I think I can feed and change and burp her without things going horribly wrong."

"How horribly wrong?" He was back to being panicked again. "What can happen? Define *wrong*."

"John." She sighed. "She's a baby. They cry and soak through their diapers and spit up and fuss for no reason. It says all of that is normal."

"None of that is normal." He frowned.

"For a *baby*, it is." She cradled Leslie, peering down into her little face. "When she's not all squished up and red, she looks an awful lot like a doll." Nat had never seen, let alone held, something this tiny. That it was a human was mind-boggling.

"I'll take your word for it." John gripped the kitchen counter at his back.

Nat nodded at the bottle. "Make sure it's not too hot, please."

John picked up the bottle, shook it, squirted it—sending a stream of formula all over his arm and shirt—before thrusting the bottle at her. "My lack of coffee is showing." He plucked at the front of his shirt. "It's not too hot." He shrugged, turned on the water and pulled off his shirt.

It was the first time Nat had seen John without his shirt in years. High school, tubing down the river, parties on the shore… A lifetime ago. Of course, he'd changed. But it wasn't the almost overdeveloped muscles of his lean body that captured her attention. It was the scars. So many scars—a peppering of raised skin—all along his back and left side. The scar that was visible on his face and neck continued down his chest and disappeared beneath the waist of his worn and faded jeans. It was solid, more pronounced, than the rest.

What had happened to him? The scars... Well, she didn't want to imagine it. She couldn't. The whole time he'd been deployed, she'd refused to let herself worry about all the possible dangers he faced. But now, seeing what he *had* been through... Her heart twisted, hollow and thumping against her rib cage. Had he been alone? How long had he suffered? *He is still suffering.* All she had to do was watch him move to see that. Whatever had happened hadn't just left his skin scarred, it had scarred his insides, too. She needed to remember that.

Nat took the bottle, tested it and nodded. "Perfect. Thanks, John. Your daddy is a champion bottle maker, Leslie."

John made a startled, near-choking sound.

One thing Nat wasn't ready to give up on yet: John accepting Leslie. He'd been through so much, was so alone and lost. Nat couldn't help but hope that this little bundle could help heal him. Growing up the way she had, she knew parenthood wasn't for everyone. Her mother had been a perfect example. Until Grampa Bear, Nat thought of herself as a mistake—a mistake and a nuisance that no one paid much attention to unless it was to blame her or chastise her for things she hadn't done. She'd been so scared to bring attention to herself, she'd been painfully shy when she started school in Granite Falls.

She didn't want John to have regrets when it came to his daughter. "John, you should call the doctor and schedule a paternity test. For your peace of mind."

John made a noncommittal sound but nothing else.

Whether or not he raised Leslie, John needed to make a fully informed choice about his daughter versus reacting in panic and fear.

She carried Leslie back into the living room and sat in Bear's recliner. "We'll get this all figured out, won't we?" she asked the baby, watching the tiny bow of a mouth latch onto the bottle and drink vigorously. "We will figure it all out. One day at a time."

Hearing Nat say *we* sent calm rolling over him. She might be running on fumes and suffering from some sort of motherly-surge thing, but he could not do this without her. The *we* was essential—for him. And the baby.

Baby.

A baby that was...his.

He was a father?

Not just no, but hell, no! He'd fathered a baby. He was *not* a father. Even he knew there was a huge difference between the two. He still couldn't get his mind wrapped around that one. Was it physically possible? Yes. But…but… What were the odds? *Clearly, not good.*

Nat was right: he should get a test and know for certain.

All night long he'd been trying to process what this meant. So far, he was as rattled as he was the minute Nat had told him the tiny, living, breathing, screaming thing was somehow his.

It's not like he didn't want a family. He did. A family had been in his five-year plan—when he'd still had a five-year plan. But that was before he'd lost the use of his knee and his military career. Now a plan seemed like an overwhelming waste of time. What he wanted versus what he was capable of were two entirely different things.

The therapist he'd been forced to speak to had said a whole bunch of obvious or useless stuff. One such nugget was that John needed to focus and decide what he *wanted*. He said he needed to have something to work toward—beyond physically healing. John was pretty sure the guy had no idea what he was talking about. If he did, he wouldn't have made the whole thing sound so damn easy. John knew better. It wasn't easy. His life was far from easy… And that was before a baby had turned up at his front door.

Your daddy… Nat said it with such assurance. Him, a father? *Poor kid.* Assuming Leslie was his.

He glanced over the counter that was the official delineator between the kitchen and living room. Bear's supersized recliner was rocking but he couldn't see Nat or the baby. He could hear them. Nat humming Aerosmith and the baby gurgling and smacking. It was surprisingly peaceful. Until Leslie needed burping. Then things got dicey.

He picked up the phone, dialed Emily's number and frowned as it went straight to voice mail. "Emily, it's John again. I'd appreciate a call back. I… I realize this is a difficult situation, but I'd like to discuss options together. Please give me a call." He hung up and rubbed a hand over his face.

Nat was changing Leslie, the pitch and volume of Leslie's cries making him wince.

"How can something so little make so much noise?" He tugged on his earlobe.

Nat didn't hear him—how could she? He watched, marveling at how easy Nat made this whole thing look. She wasn't wincing or panicking or running, screaming, from the house… Nope, one tiny diaper aside, a new one in place, and Leslie was back to being all wound up neatly in the blanket-cocoon thing Nat had worked out. Most importantly, the house was quiet.

Nat glanced his way, a small smile on her face, as she rested her cheek on the top of Leslie's down-covered head. "Not too shabby, eh?"

"Nope," he murmured.

Nat was tired, in pink motorcycle pajamas, with bruise-like shadows under her blue eyes, and her short and sassy dark hair was going every which way, but to him, she looked…beautiful. He swallowed. *Damn beautiful.*

Where the hell had that come from?

He was sleep-deprived, too, that's all. Last night had been a never-ending series of diaper changes, screaming fits and panic attacks.

Yes, Nat was a good-looking woman, but he wasn't about to start thinking about her as anything other than Nat. His friend. His confidante. His go-to, no matter what. He wasn't suddenly going to view her as a *woman* woman. One with curves that would have made him hungry for her—if she wasn't Nat, that is. And her eyes? Deep and blue and warm… What would it be like to see an invitation in those eyes?

"John?" Nat was saying, looking at him with open concern.

"Sorry." He ran a hand over his face, wiping away the all-too-tempting picture of Nat smiling up at him, eager for his kiss. He cleared his throat. "What?"

"I said we're on the brink of a situation here."

She nodded at the bag. "Diapers. We're almost out."

John eyed the three tiny white rectangles sitting beside the box Leslie was using for a bed. "Oh." *Dammit.* "Well…" He shook his head. "We can't exactly do without."

"No." Nat sighed. "So…a trip into town? Who's going? Who's staying?"

Granite Falls Family Grocery store. There was no way he was going there. None. He'd drive the extra twenty miles to Johnson City and get diapers there, where the chances of him being recognized were slim to none.

The other alternative? Staying here with Leslie?

"I'll go," he offered.

"Can you drive okay?" she asked, hesitating. "It won't bother you?"

The rain-induced flair of arthritis had eased some, but he'd be lying if he said it didn't still hurt like a son of a bitch. "You use your right leg to drive," he teased. "If you're using your left leg, you're doing it wrong."

Nat smiled. "Look at you, being all sassy."

"You're good?" he asked. "With Alpha and Leslie?"

"You are planning on coming back? With diapers?" She was joking, but she did wait for him to nod before she went on. "Then, as long as you don't take *too* long, we should survive. You might as well get formula, too. And baby wipes… I'll make a list." She headed into the kitchen, writing down what was needed, and handed it to him.

He scanned the list, appreciating the brand of formula and diaper size she'd included. "Anything else?"

"Coffee."

He chuckled. "Right." He added it. "I'll get going." He owed Nat, big-time. If she needed coffee, he'd get it for her. *Whatever* she needed, whatever she wanted, he'd give it to her. Starting now.

Chapter Six

Nat was pacing the floor, alternating between patting and rocking a fussy Leslie, when she heard the knock on the front door. John wouldn't knock, would he? And it wasn't like the door was locked.

Emily?

Nat stood there, her heart in her throat. Of course, Emily would come back for her daughter. She'd had more than twenty-four hours to herself, she'd thought things through and she'd come back.

So why wasn't Nat ecstatic? Why wasn't she running to the door?

Alpha sat, his head cocking to one side as the knocking grew more insistent.

"I know," she said, sighing. "I'm just surprised."

She shifted Leslie, drew in a deep breath and slowly walked toward the front door. But the moment she opened the door she saw it wasn't Emily and it wasn't John…

"Jan?" she asked, beyond surprised. *I can do this. I can do this.* Her stomach rolled, churning and gurgling. *I don't know if I can do this.*

"Natalie," Jan smiled, a casserole dish in her hands. Her eyes went round the moment she saw the tiny, squirming presence of Leslie. "Who is this?"

"This is Leslie." Nat was frozen. *Your grand-daughter.* What was she supposed to do? *What am I supposed to say?* What if John came home? Or Emily showed up? Or called. *This is a nightmare.*

"Can I come in?" Jan asked. "I won't stay long. After we ran into each other at the grocery store, I felt the need to visit. You being on your own and all." She paused, smiling at the baby. "At least, I thought you were alone."

Nat stepped aside for Jan. "Yes, please come in." She was certain the older woman heard the waver in her voice—if not the thud-thud of her speeding heart.

Jan stepped inside, clearly curious. "And who is this?" She smiled at Alpha. "Aren't you a hand-some fella?"

Alpha's tail thumped in greeting.

"This is Alpha." Nat swallowed. Did Jan know her son had a dog named Alpha? Her stomach clenched. More gurgles.

Jan didn't ignore the monster-movie-like sound Nat's stomach was continuing to make. "Are you all right, Nat? You look awful pale." The older woman's hand rested on Nat's arm, all motherly concern.

"Yes." *No. Not in the least.* "I'm just…" *Trying not to throw up.* "Babies. You know." She laughed—there was nothing natural about the laugh. "They're exhausting." *Calm.*

Jan's gaze was fixed on her face now, her brow creasing. "Where is her mother?"

Stick to the truth. "She needed a break." Nat shrugged, shifting Leslie in her arms. "She…she's considering giving Leslie up for adoption, so I'm keeping the baby until she's figured out what she needs to do." She swallowed. "It's a…*difficult* situation." Nat almost laughed again.

"Oh." Jan's brows rose. Her curiosity shifted to concern. "Is there no father in the picture, then?"

"Not really." *Your son, Leslie's father, is in the picture, but he doesn't want to be.* Nat knew, she just knew, Jan would be devastated when she learned all the details of…everything. *It's not my news to give.* "As far as I know, he's only just found out."

"Poor little thing." Jan's hand rested on Leslie's back. "Can I hold her? I'd be happy to give you a break. Taking care of Hayden's Weston, and Kyle and Skylar's little Greer was like a baby-refresher course." She chuckled.

Of course you can hold your granddaughter. Nat swallowed once, then again. "That would be wonderful."

"Let me put this down." Jan carried the casserole into the kitchen, her gaze making a quick sweeping assessment of the room.

Mail stacked on the table alongside formula and bottle paraphernalia.

An overturned diaper bag next to Leslie's car seat.

No big deal.

But the milk crate full of empty beer bottles Nat was planning to take to the recycling center *and* the blanket on the couch—plus John's empty beer bottle from last night on the floor—definitely didn't look good.

Last, but not least, Jan saw the *Bringing Up Baby* book and peered into the banker's box. Rather, the box Leslie was using as a bed.

Whatever Jan was thinking, she kept it to herself. Instead, she slid the casserole dish onto the counter and turned. "Let me wash my hands real quick."

The minute Leslie was in Jan's arms, Nat got to work. She had never been a house-proud person, but she was a stickler for keeping things neat, tidy and clean. And right now, the house was none of those things. She put the milk crate of beer bottles on the back porch, cleaned the kitchen, folded John's blanket, then neatly stacked the letters and placed them in a basket with the IRS letter buried on the bottom.

"Nat." Jan sat at the kitchen table, rocking Leslie in her arms. "Is everything okay?"

Considering the circumstances, it wasn't an unfair question to ask. *Because I look like I'm exhausted and a mess and I'm taking care of a random baby—on my own?* "I'm fine, Jan. I promise."

Jan didn't buy it. How could she? *Between the beer bottles and the baby-box bed…*

"It's very kind of you to help out your friend with Leslie," Jan said, glancing down at the infant. The baby was sleeping peacefully. "She is a tiny thing. How old is she?"

"She's almost a month." There had been an envelope tucked into the car seat with Leslie's shot record and a copy of her hospital records, too.

"A month?" Jan repeated, cradling Leslie. "The first three months can be a challenge." She smiled up at Nat. "Hayden was all fusses and gas. He'd wriggle and grunt and cry until his father, my Pete, worried he'd make himself sick. Kyle was pretty easy-going—he could sleep through anything, and he was always hungry." She sighed. "But John. Well, he was a mix of both. Even as a baby, he was sweet and smiling one minute, then red-faced and bellowing the next. I guess he hasn't changed all that much." She glanced at Nat. "When will Leslie's mother come back?"

"Oh…" Nat ran a hand over her hair, realizing just how disheveled she must look. Messy hair, pink motorcycle pajamas—with a spattering of formula spit-up over her right shoulder, and who knew how bloodshot her eyes were. *On top of the beer bottles and the box-baby bed.* "A week."

"Are you taking a week off?" Jan asked.

Because the only thing worse than fortysomething empty beer bottles and a box baby-bed would be taking one-month old Leslie to work with her at the bar. "Yes." She smiled. "I can't exactly take her to work." She laughed, again. *Way to sound unhinged.*

Jan was studying the baby, but Nat knew the woman was coming up with just the right thing to say. "I'd like to help out, Nat. I have a bit of experience with babies, after all. And I know this is all new to you," she said, nodding at the baby book. "Plus, we have a few hand-me-down baby items you're welcome to use while Leslie is here. My grandbabies are all a bit bigger now."

Not all of them. Leslie is your granddaughter. This is John's daughter. Nat wanted to cry. And throw up. And take a nap. "I couldn't ask you to do that—"

"You're not asking." Jan shook her head. "I'm offering. Now—" she gave Nat a gentle smile "—how about you go take a shower, give yourself a minute and we'll figure some sort of schedule out when you're done."

A shower does sound like heaven. She glanced

at the clock. John could be home any minute—
with the much-needed diapers. And if that happened? What then? Would it be awkward? Yes.
But not bad. Jan loved her son—she missed him.
John would finally have to face his mother. John
would have to tell her…everything. And all the
lies and secrets she was keeping would be over. *I
do need a shower.*

"I promise, we will be just fine." Jan smiled.
"While Leslie naps, Alpha and I can have a chat—
just us old-timers—and you can enjoy a few minutes to yourself."

"Are you sure?" She needed a shower, so why
was she feeling so guilty?

"I'm absolutely certain." Jan nodded.

"Thank you, Jan." Nat paused. "I'm grateful
you stopped by, and thank you for the food and
the extra set of hands."

"It is my pleasure, Natalie." She seemed to hesitate. "I'm trying not to worry over the beer."

"Please don't." She shook her head. *Stick to the
truth.* Well, as close as possible. "I'm not the one
drinking it. I have another friend who's been dealing with things—not too well, obviously. I'm hoping he'll pull himself together, but for now, I've
been letting him stay."

"You're so kindhearted." Jan shook her head.
"Just like Bear. That man never turned a soul
away."

Nat swallowed down the lump in her throat, her eyes stinging. Grampa Bear always had a place at the table for whoever needed it. But he'd never, ever be okay with the amount of lying going on. He'd said, over and over, to be careful with words and only say what was necessary and kind. Honesty was something Grampa Bear took seriously. *No matter how hard it might be to say or hear, the only right answer is the honest one.*

"I'll be quick," Nat said, hurrying from the kitchen before the tears she was holding back managed to slip free. She didn't mind crying—it helped get things out. But this time she worried that, once she started, she wouldn't be able to stop.

She gathered some clean clothes, rushed to the bathroom and turned on the hot water. *Hurry home, John. It's time for you to come clean and sort out your messes.* But it wasn't just John anymore… And the person she was most worried about now wasn't John at all. It was Leslie. Leslie was a baby. She needed protection, care…and love. There was so much love in the Mitchell family. The reason this feud with Hayden weighed so heavily on John was because he loved his big brother so much. Grampa Bear said the brothers needed time locked in a room together. He said they'd either hug it out or fight it out, but either way, it'd fix things.

But there was no quick fix when it came to

Leslie. If only there was some way she could get through to John, to make him understand that giving up Leslie was a forever thing. Something that could turn into a forever regret. She didn't want that for John…or Leslie. But what she wanted wouldn't change a thing. This was John's decision, John's life, and John's baby, and the sooner she accepted that, the better.

John rolled into the driveway when the sun was low on the horizon. His shirt was streaked with grease, and there was a rip in the knee of his jeans. Nothing like having a blowout on the side of the road in the fading light of the sun to end your day. He was hot and irritated and filthy—not to mention hurting from the pain in his knee—and he knew he'd be greeted with Leslie's banshee-wails and Nat's anger over how late he was.

I have the diapers. And every other damn thing on the list, too.

He was surprised by the sound he heard when he was halfway up the path to the front door. Nothing. Absolute silence. The lack of noise continued all the way to the door. He opened it, bracing himself… Nothing.

He didn't know whether to be relieved or concerned.

When he crept into the kitchen, he stopped short. Everything was clean. *Clean* clean. Like a deep-scrubbing sort of thing. He turned, surveying the kitchen and living room. There was no evidence that he or Leslie were staying there. No empty beer bottles, no bottles or formula, no blanket on the couch—nothing. The house looked as it did the day he'd arrived.

"Hello?" he called out, growing increasingly more concerned by the long silence. "Nat?"

"In the back room." Nat's voice was light and breezy and not at all irritated or stressed.

That makes one of us. A mix of relief and wariness spun in his stomach as he set the groceries on the counter. He was late, very late, and Nat— and Leslie—had every right to be upset about it. Taking a deep breath, he headed down the hall, uncertain of the reception he'd get.

What greeted him had him scratching his head. Nat? Standing in the middle of…a nursery? "How the hell long was I gone?" He made a show of rubbing his eyes as he stared around the room. "And what the hell happened?" he asked, staring around the room Bear had once used to work on his military-vehicle models. *No sign of those now.*

"You were gone so long I was beginning to think you'd forgotten your way back." Nat, who was changing Leslie's diaper, smiled as she glanced his way. "Well…your mother stopped by."

John blinked, the spinning in his stomach increasing. "Wait, what?" He swallowed hard. "My mother?"

"She dropped by…" She stopped and gave him a once-over, a furrow marring her brow. "What happened to you?"

"Blowout," he said, waving that aside. "My mother was here?" His mother had done this? Did she know he was here? About Leslie? All he managed to get out was "*She* did this?"

"She did." Nat frowned at his stained shirt and torn jeans, but she nodded slowly. "People are talking…about me. I'm getting somewhat of a reputation for all the beer I've been buying. She came out to make sure I was okay." Nat did the blanket-wrap thing on Leslie, scooped up the baby and carefully placed her in the new crib before her blue eyes met his. "She took one look at the mess and empty beer bottles and baby box and was pretty sure things weren't okay so…she did this. You know your mom, John. She has a big heart."

He did know his mother. This was just the sort of thing she'd do for Nat. For anyone in need. The other bit, about Nat being talked about? Guilt landed a hard blow to his chest. It wasn't right that he'd put Nat in that situation. He'd no doubt Nat had told his mother everything. Why wouldn't she? It was a lot. All of this. He'd been asking too much of Nat, for too long. Now that his secret was out, he tried to brace himself for what was to come. "What did you tell her?"

"Nothing." She swallowed. "It was awful. I looked your mother in the eye and lied to her. Even though she let me take a shower and brought over the changing table and crib for Leslie—and stopped and bought diapers, too." There was a hint of reprimand in her voice. "I lied to her, and the moment she left, I got sick."

John felt like a bastard then. "I'm sorry, Nat." He crossed the room, not stopping until he had her in his arms.

"No, you're not." Her voice was muffled against his shoulder. "You're just relieved she believed me so you don't have to face her."

There was no point arguing; she was right. Facing his mother would have been...*hard*. "That, too," he agreed, burying his nose against the softness of her hair. "But I am sorry. I know you've done...everything. And I haven't exactly—"

"Helped." Her voice wavered. "Not much. Not enough." Her arms slid around his back. "But I need help." She was crying now, little hiccupy sobs that reached into his chest and put a vise around his heart. He'd made her cry. Nat. His Nat.

"I know." He tightened his hold. "Don't cry." She was right. She'd cooked and cleaned and never asked a thing of him, even after working a full day. And that was *before* Leslie had shown up.

"I've been a selfish bastard, Nat. I have. But I'll do better."

She snorted.

"Ouch." Her quick dismissal hurt. *I deserve it*. Why the hell should she believe him? All he knew was he couldn't bear to see her this way. Nat was the one he could count on to smile her way through anything. She was the motivator, the one who could inspire you to get up no matter how many times you'd been knocked down. How did he repay her? By wearing her out, asking too much and making her cry. All when she had her own problems to deal with. Since Leslie's arrival, he'd forgotten all about the IRS letter. *Because I am a selfish bastard*. "Don't cry," he murmured again against her temple. "I'm not worth your tears, Nat."

She pulled back. "Stop it, John Mitchell. You stop that." She pushed against his chest. "You don't get to say things like that, not to me."

He held on to her, watching her temper flare. He didn't want her mad at him, but it was better than her tears.

"You don't get to tell me how to feel about you, you hear me?" She gripped the front of his shirt and gave him a little shake—not that he actually moved. "I know who you are and what you're capable of. Just because you've forgotten doesn't mean I have."

He knew better. "What I *was* capable of—"

"No, John," she cut him off. "What you are capable of. I've never known anyone as stubborn as you." She smoothed his shirt. "Maybe Grampa Bear but… If someone said you couldn't do something, you went out of your way to prove them wrong. When there was a football, track or bronc-riding record, you didn't stop until you'd broken it. It's who you are. A fighter. An irritating, competitive, in-your-face, challenge-accepted, charming, too-handsome-for-your-own-good, hard-working, determined fighter. If there was ever a time to use that stubborn fight, it'd be now. Find it, John. Somehow. I know it's there, inside. I know it." She pressed against him again.

He got lost in those blue eyes somewhere around *too-handsome*… Nat thought he was handsome? She'd more or less hurled that and a whole slew of praises at him like a laundry list of insults, but he'd heard her say it. Nat believed in him. *And she thinks I'm handsome.*

"John?" She was so angry. All flushed and shaking.

John went from surprise to mounting panic. Little things like the feel of Nat's heartbeat, racing, against his chest. The swell of her pink lower lip. The hint of spearmint clinging to her silky-soft hair, where he'd buried his nose minutes before. Awareness teased along his every nerve ending until he was scrambling to recover. He didn't want to feel this way about Nat. He sure as hell didn't want Nat to be this fiery woman with curves that made him weak-kneed.

He needed her to put on some denim overalls—and quick.

She seemed to pick up on his mood, because she got real quiet, real fast. Those blue eyes went from fiery to wary, and she sort of leaned away from him.

Good. She didn't like this, either. He eased his arm from around her waist—despite the fact that he liked it right where it was. Holding her close. *What is wrong with me?* There was a line he could never cross with Nat. No matter how tempted he might be. He stepped back then, like he'd been burned. "So...so my mom..." He cleared his throat. "She was here?" *She'd already said so.* Why was he so rattled? What the hell was happening?

Nat nodded.

"I didn't think about the beer." He shook his head. His plan to make peace with Hayden had backfired, and he'd let it derail everything. Somehow, Nat had wound up bearing the brunt of that. "I haven't been thinking about a lot, I guess." He risked a glance her way. "I *am* sorry, Nat."

Those blue eyes were still pinned on him. But she wasn't angry or wary anymore. Now she was... What? What was that look? He knew. *Dammit all.* He knew. From the instant heat coiling in the pit of his belly and the tangible need to reach for her, there was no denying what this was.

Want. Damn it all if he didn't feel the same, rolling over him white-hot and urgent. *No, dammit.* This wasn't right. He and Nat… *No.* He sucked in a deep breath but couldn't tear his gaze away. The longing coursing through his blood was too powerful.

"I told her Leslie was a friend's baby." Nat spoke rapidly, forcing her attention to the crib. "I told her that the mother was considering adoption and needed some time to figure things out." She hugged herself, chattering on, as rattled as he was. "Your mother was…well, she's pretty amazing. But you know that. She took one look at the place, beer bottles and mess and all, and made up her mind she was going to help." She shook her head. "I've never seen anything like it."

You've done the same thing. She'd opened her door to him without a single question. Who else would have done that? No one. Not even his mother. The questions would have come bubbling up, whether she wanted them to or not. Nat hadn't pushed.

"She left and came back with the changing table and the crib and a baby monitor and some diapers Skylar and Kyle's youngest have outgrown." She sighed.

John had yet to meet the women, with three

children, who'd become Kyle's family. He'd missed so much. In the ten months since his discharge, he'd wallowed in self-pity and robbed himself of time he could have spent getting to know the people that were now family. He couldn't blame it all on Hayden; he knew better. His accident, his leg, his discharge… All of it was his fault. It was facing his family, all of them, as the failure they all knew him to be.

"I tried to pay her, but she wouldn't hear anything about that." Nat shook her head. "The thing is she wants to help. She knows I need to work, and she said she'd babysit so I could." She swallowed. "I put her off for now, but if Emily doesn't call soon—"

"I'll call again." John turned on his heel and headed to the kitchen for the phone, Nat following. He dialed, waited and ran a hand over his face when Emily's voice mail picked up. "Emily. Call me."

"Well, gosh, if that doesn't get her to call, I don't know what will." Nat shook her head, but she was smiling.

"Where is…she?" he asked, confused by the absence of the blanket-wrapped baby that had been in Nat's arms for the last thirty or so hours.

"She is sleeping in the crib." Nat lifted her shirt to show a walkie-talkie-like device clipped onto the waist of her jeans. "If she needs something, we will hear."

"Oh, I wasn't worried about hearing her." John leaned against the counter, instantly drained.

"You okay?" Nat asked, eyeing his shirt and jeans once more. "I'm sorry about the tire. That's never fun. And tires aren't cheap." She winced.

Especially if you're having money problems. Money problems, as in possible property seizure and owing back taxes. Here they were, both struggling with life-altering situations, and yet, to look at Nat, you'd never know. She was tough; he only pretended to be. "It's fine."

"Still, you could have been hurt—"

"I wasn't." He grinned. "But I'm touched that you care."

She rolled her eyes. "Really? I didn't think there was a question about whether or not I cared, John." She sighed for added effect. "I'd think that was obvious."

"It is." He kept on grinning. "You're my North Star, Nat. Always have been. Ever fixed. There. Reliable."

"That's me." She seemed to wilt a little. "Reliable and there."

He chuckled. "You make it sound like a bad thing."

"Did you not hear how...pathetic that sounded?"

She shrugged. "It doesn't matter. I'm going to make dinner before Leslie—"

"Banshee Baby," he interrupted.

Nat scowled. "—*Leslie* wakes up and wants her dinner."

"You might not want to turn up the volume on that thing too much, or she'll blow out the speaker when she starts to wail." He raised both eyebrows.

"John, she's a baby." Nat shook her head.

"Yep. A banshee baby." He nodded.

"Stop." But there was a slight smile on her face. "How about you peel some carrots?"

"What are we having?" he asked, opening the refrigerator.

"Stew?" She stood at his side, peering into the refrigerator.

"Sounds good." He found himself all too aware of her closeness. Her warmth. That spearmint-clean scent. The sweep of her eyelashes and her dark brow—furrowed now that she was assessing the contents of the refrigerator. He was not going to let his gaze wander along the column of her throat or along the ridge of her collarbone.

Her gaze swiveled his way.

The moment their gazes collided, the kitchen seemed to shrink, closing in on them until he was fully snared by those blue-blue eyes. Dammit all, but he didn't mind. Not in the least. He sort of liked the way she was looking at him… It was the way she'd always looked at him. As far back as he could remember, Nat had seen him as something special. He didn't know why, especially now, but there were times that look made him want to *be* something special.

Her gaze pulled free. "You should take a shower and clean up since Leslie is sleeping. Then we'll get started on the stew."

He cleared his throat. "Right." Shower. Clean Up. "Before the banshee starts a-wailing."

"Stop." Nat pushed him, her reluctant smile knocking the air from his lungs. "Go on. I'll see if I can find a patch for that hole in the knee, too."

He caught her hand. "Thanks, Nat. I honestly don't know what I'd do without you."

She tried to tug her hand free. "Yeah, yeah, I'm not going to make you take care of Leslie alone, so you don't need to butter me up—"

"I'm not." He sighed. "I mean it." He didn't blame her for being skeptical, but he hated that he'd done this—and he had. His word didn't mean as much as it used to. "No ulterior motive. Just… thank you."

She blinked once, then again. "You're welcome."

"I'll go wash up." He winked. "I'll keep an ear out for the banshee wail—in case you need back up."

"Keep it up, and I might just let you take care of

her tonight." She crossed her arms over her chest, her brows rising.

He held his hands up in defeat. "Hey, hey, I did have to change a tire on the side of the road, you know. In the dark, practically… It's not like I've been lying around on the couch all day doing nothing… Not this time, anyway." With a final wink, he left the kitchen and headed down the hall to the small guest room he'd been using. He found clean clothes, tugged off his shirt, kicked off his boots and headed out into the hallway to the bathroom, only to slam into Nat.

Chapter Seven

It wasn't the first time she'd been in John's arms today... It was the first time she'd been in his arms when he was shirtless.

"Oops," she murmured, trying not to stare at her hands—resting on John's bare chest.

Muscles... So many muscles...

"Oops?" John repeated. "Did you need something?"

Did I need something? Before she'd been distracted by the smooth, wall of muscle that was John's chest, she'd had a purpose... *Which was?*

His brows dipped, and he tilted her chin up. "Nat? What's up?"

This is worse. Not only were her hands soaking up his fabulous warmth, she was staring up and into those heavy-lidded tawny eyes—her heartbeat accelerating by the second. His expression cleared, the puzzled brow smoothing, and his gaze becoming intense enough to press all the air from her lungs. *Not breathing. Not at all.*

She was torn between stepping away, break-

ing this connection and returning to reality or…
or not stepping away. Her heart was thundering
along now.

John would stop. He'd put space between them.
Any minute now. Instead, his fingers smoothed her
hair behind her ear, and his hand rested along the
side of her face. "Nat…" The low rumble of his
voice sent a shudder down the length of her spine.

John. She swallowed. How many times had she
imagined this, right here, the tingles and touching and longing coursing through her veins? *This*
can't *happen.* No matter how much she wanted
this—wanted him—she knew better. Giving in
to John would change everything. *More like ruin
everything…*

John didn't have the best track record with
women. He was a love 'em and leave 'em sort of
fella. Leslie was proof enough of that. As much
as she wanted him to love her—really love her—
she didn't want him to leave her. She only had
one choice…

Think. She needed to stop being all moony-eyed
and ridiculous. *This can't happen.*

She'd followed him for a reason… One that she
finally remembered. *Right.* "Grampa Bear had a
therapy bath." She stepped back, pushing off his
chest with all her might and bouncing off the wall
behind her. *Smooth.* She plowed forward, determined to sever the thrum pulling them together.

"You… I don't know why I didn't think about it before. For you. Your leg. Your knee."

John's jaw muscle rippled.

"It could make a difference." She swallowed, refusing to let her gaze dip below his chin. Admiring his shirtlessness wouldn't help with her whole *this can't happen* decision. "And I think there's some of the oil left, too. His home health worker used it on his lower back. Nothing like four major motorcycle accidents to take a toll on the body." Her smile was forced. "But maybe it will help your knee, too?"

"I doubt it." The words were firm but without bite.

"Would you… Can you try?" She took a deep breath. "It could work wonders. Grampa Bear loved the thing. Please?"

His jaw muscle twitched.

"You were going to take a shower, anyway," she pointed out. "So take a therapeutic bath with power jets and bubbles instead. If it does any good, then…awesome. If not, well…you're still clean, right?"

The corner of his mouth kicked up. "Right."

"Good." She opened Bear's bedroom door, unused since his passing. "You know, you could move in here, if you want more room." She headed into the bathroom and bent over the tub. "Then you could use the bath whenever you want."

"If it works," he said, leaning against the door frame and crossing his arms over his big, broad, muscular chest…

"I'm glad you're keeping an open mind about this." She shook her head and pointed at the massive bath. "He spent a fortune on the thing—and it has a warrantee, so it better work." She sighed. "Just give it a chance, will you?"

"I'm here, aren't I?"

"And you sound thrilled." She turned on the water.

"Why haven't you moved in here?" he asked. "It's a bigger room."

"It's not my room." She shrugged, running her fingers under the water to gauge the temperature. "It's nice and hot."

"You know I can do that, right?" But he was smiling.

"I'm trying to help." She shrugged again, secretly suspecting he wouldn't take a bath if she wasn't forcing him. "All you have to do it press that button." She pointed at the panel of knobs on the wall. "Those are for the different settings, so you can figure out what works best for you." She stepped back.

"You going to help me get into the bath, too?"

"Do you need help?" she asked, suddenly horrified. "John, I'm sorry… I didn't think about getting in and out—"

"I was being a smart-ass, Nat." He sighed. "I mean, if you want to stay, feel free."

She glanced at him. "I'm pretty sure you can take it from here." And she needed to leave before her insides melted along with her self-control. With an odd, fluttering wave, she headed for the door.

He grabbed her hand as she brushed past. "Thanks again, Nat. You keep taking care of me. I don't know why, but you do."

Because I love you. She shrugged. "I don't, either." *I've always loved you.* For someone who said they could always tell when she was lying, it was ironic that he didn't see through her on this. Maybe he didn't want to see the truth. Maybe, like her, he wasn't willing to sacrifice what they had for something more. "Oh." She turned, stooped to rifle under the sink, searching for the arnica massage oil Grampa Bear swore by. "Wait…" She pushed aside a box of dental floss—Grampa Bear was all about dental floss. "Here it is." She grabbed the bottle and set it on the counter. "Right after your bath, while your skin's still warm and damp." The words conjured up an all-too-tempting image. If she thought John's chest was appealing now, she could only imagine the added effect of water and oil and… It was time to slam on the mental brakes and get out of here. *Don't look at him.* She headed for the door. *Don't look at him.*

By the time she'd closed herself in Grampa

Bear's room, she was shaking. Her mental brakes had failed, and her mind was literally spinning with an array of delectable bad ideas that all included John in various stages of undress.

Alpha stood, tail wagging, looking up at her.

"Hi," she said, breathless. "I'm in trouble, Alpha. Big trouble."

Alpha cocked his head to one side.

"No, I mean it." She covered her face with her hands. "I don't have time for this…" As tired as she was, there was no point in trying to sleep. If inappropriate thoughts of John didn't distract her, Leslie's imminent wake-up would. "Laundry." She gave Alpha a scratch behind the ear. "We'll do some laundry, and we'll have some tea on the porch before we get started on dinner." If Leslie hadn't woken up.

Once the washer was full, and she had a glass of iced tea in hand, she and Alpha made their way to the porch. "I'm finally going to get a turn in my—" She broke off.

Vlad sat back in the swing—at ease—crunching on what looked an awful lot like Alpha's dog food.

"Really?" she asked the raccoon. "What, do you hang out at windows, listening for me so you can hop right in there before I can?"

Vlad showed her his teeth, then went back to eating.

Alpha, who tended to ignore Vlad, sniffed the

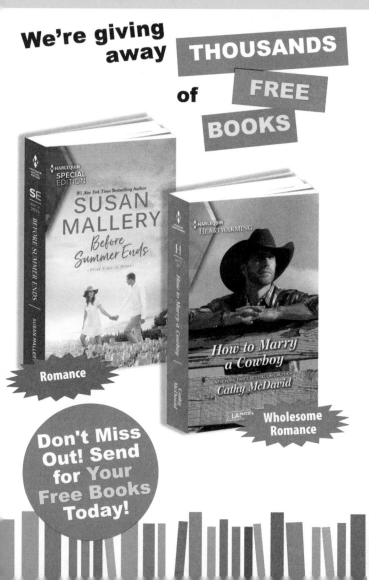

Get up to 4
FREE FABULOUS BOOKS
You Love!

To thank you for being a loyal reader we'd like to send you up to 4 FREE BOOKS, absolutely free.

Just write "YES" on the Loyal Reader Voucher and we'll send you up to 4 Free Books and Free Mystery Gifts, altogether worth over $20, as a way of saying thank you for being a loyal reader.

Try **Harlequin® Special Edition** books featuring comfort and strength in the support of loved ones and enjoying the journey no matter what life throws your way.

Try **Harlequin® Heartwarming™ Larger-Print** books featuring uplifting stories where the bonds of friendship, family and community unite.

Or **TRY BOTH!**

We are so glad you love the books as much as we do and can't wait to send you great new books.

So don't miss out, return your Loyal Reader Voucher Today!

Pam Powers

LOYAL READER
FREE BOOKS VOUCHER

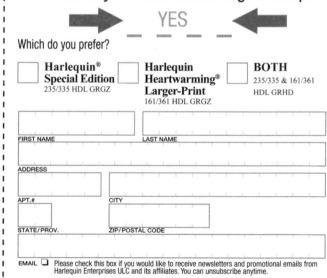

air. He ambled over to the swing, his massive head crowding in on the raccoon. Alpha's low growl made the hair on the back of Nat's neck stand up, so she could only imagine how Vlad felt.

To Nat's astonishment, Vlad pushed all the dog food toward Alpha and pressed himself against the back of the swing—waiting.

Alpha sniffed the food, devoured it in one bite and turned back to Nat.

"You left one," Nat pointed out. A single piece of kibble remained. "Or were you being kind to Vlad?"

Vlad glanced back and forth between Alpha and the piece of dog food, assessing the likelihood of a trap.

"If he wanted to eat you, he'd eat you," Nat said, shaking her head at him.

Vlad made a chitter-chirp sound, snatched the dog food, leaped from the swing and moved to the far side of the porch.

Alpha sat looking up at her, tail wagging.

"If I didn't know better, I'd say you just negotiated the release of my swing for some dog food." She sat in her swing, sighing. "I have to admit it, Alpha, this is nice."

Alpha yawned, lay on the wood porch and sprawled out on his side.

"You've earned a nice long rest," Nat agreed, sipping her iced tea. "We both have." She leaned back and closed her eyes, one foot resting on the porch to keep the swing moving.

John had zero expectations and zero hope about the bath or the oil. He'd been dealing with this for long enough to know better. The long soak in a hot tub had eased some of the tightness behind his knee and along his calf. The oil, smell aside, had amplified the effect. It wouldn't last forever, but he'd take what he got. He worked through the stretches the physical therapist had given him, surprised at the difference the soak and oil made. It pulled and ached, but he managed to complete a full set without breaking a sweat. Nat would be happy to know Grampa Bear's bath did, in fact, work. He grinned as he dressed in his other pair of jeans and a button-up shirt and tugged on his soft-as-butter, worn-to-perfection cowboy boots.

"Almost civilized," he said to his reflection. If it wasn't for the few days' worth of stubble on his jaw, he'd almost be presentable. Not that he needed to get dressed up. It was just him and Nat.

Nat.

That was beginning to become quite the conundrum.

The looks.

The smiles.

The awareness.

The near constant need to touch her.

"Not a good idea," he told himself. "It's a bad idea. A very bad idea." He ran a hand along his jaw, shook his head and left the bathroom.

There was no wailing, so that was a good thing. For reasons he didn't understand, he found himself heading toward Leslie's makeshift nursery, anyway. To look in on her, that's all. If she woke up or fussed or moved, he was out of there. But she was so quiet. Was that a good thing? She was normally the opposite of quiet. He held his breath and tiptoed across the room to peer over the edge of the crib. Only then did he let out a near-silent sigh of relief.

Leslie was sound asleep. As usual, she was secured in the blanket-wrap thing Nat did. It looked uncomfortable as hell to him, but hey, if Nat thought it was the thing to do, he wasn't going to argue. She did look peaceful. Her little face was pink and smooth, not mottled and squished up. Like this, she was sort of…cute. And tiny. How the hell could anything be this tiny? It wasn't the first time he wondered if this was normal. Surely a baby shouldn't be *this* small? Leslie seemed extra small.

He snorted. *Like I have so much experience with babies.*

His snort caused a squeak.

John backed up, causing one of the wooden floorboards to creak.

Another squeak and a blanket-wrap-wriggle.

Dammit. He kept going, backing up on tiptoes until he was in the hall and moving, quickly, away. He kept right on going until he was on the front porch—catching the front screen door before it slammed shut.

Nat was sound asleep, lulled by the fading sunlight and the swaying of her hammock swing, the faint grunting and squealing barely audible through the monitor clipped to her waist.

Alpha gave him a brief look before yawning and laying his head down again.

John wasn't going to wake her up: he couldn't. Hopefully, Banshee Baby would go back to sleep, and Nat could have a nap, too. He headed for the rocking chair.

Son of a bitch.

Vlad sat, slumped against the cushions, looking ready to pounce if John dared to come any closer.

"Don't even think about it," John murmured. "She might not use the broom on you. I will."

Vlad hissed.

"Keep it up." John shook his head.

Vlad hissed and growled, with a little more oomph this time.

"You got me shaking in my boots." But the harder John looked at the grumpy vermin, the more John related to him. All Vlad wanted was his own spot, food, and peace or companionship when he wanted. From the scars on his face and the one eye, Vlad hadn't had an easy go of it. Now, with Nat, he did. "She's taking care of you, too, isn't she?"

Vlad's ears swiveled forward. No hiss. No growl. Just listening.

"Are you talking to Vlad?" Nat asked, a smile in her voice.

"No. Like I'd talk to a raccoon." John spun on his heel to find Nat stretching. Not just a little stretch, either. Nope, she had her arms up and over her head, her back arching so much that her Bear's House T-shirt was stretched tight across her breasts. Whatever wisecracks he'd been considering got trapped behind the lump in his throat. The pure abandon of that stretch. The peek at her stomach under the hem of her shirt… His pants felt far less roomy. He shoved his hands in his pockets.

"I heard you," Nat said, finishing her stretch by extending her legs out in front of her, even going so far as to point her bare toes. "I talk to him all the time, so I'm not judging you… Not about talking to Vlad, anyway." Her smile was playful. "I think animals are the best confidants. They do know how to keep a secret. So it's nice to know you have Alpha with you—that you weren't all alone dealing with…what you've had to deal with."

"We get on just fine." John shrugged. "And I think he knows I've got his back."

Nat leaned forward to rub her hand along Alpha's exposed belly. "You like that, do you?" she asked, smiling as Alpha rolled onto his back.

John shook his head. "Way to play hard-to-get, Alpha."

"Why pass up a good belly rub?" Nat crooned.

Vlad's chittering sound drew John's attention.

"Looks like a good time, doesn't it?" John chuckled, watching the way Vlad was leaning forward, studying Nat and Alpha closely. "You're a raccoon, Vlad. Not a dog. Don't go getting your hopes up."

Vlad made another chirp-click, resting his paws on the arm of the chair and rising up to see more clearly.

"You're making him jealous," John said.

"I am?" Nat asked, laughing.

"Look at him." John pointed at Vlad. "I don't know what a one-eyed, crotchety-old-man of a raccoon will do in a spurt of jealousy, *but* I'd sleep with one eye open."

Nat's blue eyes shifted from Vlad to John… Once their gazes met, John's train of thought was lost. He was starting to really like this new, way-more-feminine version of Nat minus braids or overalls. He definitely liked watching the color creep into her cheeks and the spark ignite in those blue eyes—from sky blue to blazing sapphire in a matter of seconds.

It took every ounce of self-control he had to

tear his gaze from hers, to snap the thread of anticipation holding him in its thrall. With Nat, he saw things differently. She gave him hope. Hope in life, in the future and in himself. And now, hope that—maybe—he wasn't as hard and dried up as he thought. Because, looking at Nat, his heart felt nothing but warmth and, dammit, hope. What the hell was he supposed to do with that?

Just then, the baby monitor attached to Nat's waist burst to life with startling ferocity.

Vlad went shooting out of the rocker, across the porch and up the nearest tree.

Alpha turned in several circles, finding a place in the afternoon sun to resume his nap.

"The banshee baby wakes," he said, watching Nat.

"You cannot give your daughter a nickname like that, John." She stood, stretching again. "It's not nice."

He ignored the *your daughter* comment but he couldn't ignore the fact that her T-shirt was stretched to its limits.

"Why don't you come with me?" she asked. "Some basic baby handling won't hurt you."

"But it might hurt her." He shook his head. "How about I make that stew?"

Leslie's fusses had reached epic decibels, so Nat went inside without another word. He lingered on the porch, appreciating the tranquility of Bear's home. When he'd been a boy, he'd thought this place was spooky. At the end of a dead-end street and on an oversize lot, keeping plenty of distance between his place and his neighbors. The fact that the trees and shrubs lined a portion of the fence lines and the front of the house only added to the mystique of the place.

Being here was nothing like being home.

Where Bear's place was mostly overgrown and closed-in, the Mitchell ranch was nothing but sprawling fields and rolling hills. Acres and acres of wide-open spaces. If the rain was plentiful, the grass was emerald green and lush. Wildflowers. A cold stream that cut through behind the house just right for summer picnics and cookouts. Burning cedar bonfires on cold nights. Riding horses for hours, bringing in strays and checking fence wires for hours…

It was the idea of him, trying to ride, that brought his reminiscing to a stop. What the hell sort of cowboy would he be if he couldn't even ride a damn horse anymore?

He pushed off the porch railing and headed inside.

Until this whole thing with Leslie was sorted out, he was at a standstill. No point in thinking about home or what he could or couldn't do. Nat had Banshee Baby under control. He'd throw together a stew, and they'd go on. One thing at a time.

For now, he'd soak up the little everyday things. Fresh coffee. The rocker on the porch. Arguing with an ornery raccoon. Giving Alpha a good rubdown. Nat, singing rock anthems to Leslie for lullabies. Nat's smile or her stretches or her eye rolls or her optimistic spin on everything.

Damn... She was so good at carrying the weight of the world on her shoulders, he kept forgetting about the letter from the IRS. Unlike his return home, the IRS wouldn't wait. He knew Nat was proud and strong and independent, but if there was something he could do to help, he wanted to. It wasn't just about owing her, either... It was something else. The last few days, that something was damn near impossible to overlook. The surge of anticipation that rose up inside him when her blue eyes looked his way. The need to smile when she did. Watching her talk to Vlad or Alpha or Leslie like, at any minute, they'd say something back to her... All those things made it impossible for him to stay glued to the couch, hating Lt. Rogers, his knee and his big brother. If he was being honest with himself, his time with Natalie was showing him some things he wasn't all that proud of. No matter what he threw at her or how belligerent or lazy he'd been, she'd kept her cool. For a time, that had rattled him, making him push her even more. It wasn't intentional: he hadn't even realized he was doing it until she'd broken down in his arms.

Nat had never done a single bad thing to him his entire life, and he was still justifying ways to test her. Why?

Maybe he needed to spend less time being right and blaming others and more time thinking things through before he reacted.

The faint hummed notes of Def Leppard's "Pour Some Sugar on Me" reached him. He turned, smiling. How could anyone turn such a raunchy song into such a sweet-sounding melody? Leave it to Nat to do just that. The baby monitor sat on the table, the lights blinking when her humming got pitchy or louder.

"Look at you, all clean and perfect." Nat's voice was gentle. "Are you ready for your bottle? Let's go get one."

Leslie fussed a little.

"Don't worry. Everything will be okay. I promise I'll do my best to make sure you end up with a momma and a daddy who will want you and love you with their whole hearts, little one."

John's heart turned over in his chest. Once, when he and his brother Kyle and Buzz Lafferty had been kids up to no good and hiding beneath the bleachers at one of the rodeos, he'd overheard a little about what Nat's life had been before she'd come to Granite Falls. Even as a child, it'd turned John's blood cold. How Nat had been skinny and malnourished and bruised and jumpier than a cat on a hot tin roof when she'd arrived on Bear's front porch. John had been young, but over the years, he'd put two and two together. When Nat's mother was alive and well, she'd made certain Nat knew she wasn't wanted—verbally and physically. Now here she was, promising a baby who might be *his* daughter she'd do her best to give Leslie a loving family so his baby didn't grow up like Nat had.

For the first time in months, John wished he was that man. A solid, reliable, nurturing man a child could always count on. A good father. He wished he had it in him to do right by Leslie—to be the father Nat wanted for his little girl. Even if he wanted to, there was no way he could do it alone, and he was alone.

First things first, he needed to confirm Leslie was his. Then, he'd do what was best for Leslie—that meant helping Nat find good parents for her. People who could give this little girl everything he couldn't. It was the right thing to do—for everyone. So he was surprised by the hard twist in his stomach and the sharp tug in his chest at the thought of someone else humming lullabies to his banshee baby.

Chapter Eight

Nat had never intended to fall in love with Leslie. She'd learned the importance of self-preservation at an early age—and the easiest way to do that was not to get too attached or invested. Up until Leslie, only two people had been the exception to that: Grampa Bear and John. But now… Well, in the week that Leslie had been with her, she'd moved right in and taken up residence in Nat's heart.

Every time the phone rang, Nat was filled with dread. Emily hadn't called or answered any of John's calls—yet. But that could change. It had to. Sooner or later, Emily would realize what she was giving up and come back for her precious little girl. Nat wasn't saying caring for a newborn was easy—it wasn't—but it was the most rewarding thing Nat had ever experienced. Teaching John how to care for a newborn? That was the real trial. Though she had to give him credit—he was trying.

That afternoon, John had an appointment for a paternity test, and, tomorrow, Nat was finally going back to work at the Bear's House. Things were going to get interesting.

"You don't think Walt and Rebecca can handle things?" John asked for the millionth time, trailing after her as she collected the mail from the old metal mailbox along the curb.

"Walt and Rebecca have been handling things, John. I know my part-timers, Marcy and Clem, have enjoyed the extra hours but… Well, extra hours aren't free." Money was in short supply right now. Her week with Leslie had enabled her to ignore things she shouldn't be ignoring. Like the IRS, the debt and her very uncertain future. She sighed, pulling the pile of letters, flyers and one ominous-looking packet from the mailbox. *Speak of the devil…er, IRS.*

"I sound all kinds of ungrateful. Sorry, Nat." John's tone was soft, catching her attention.

"It's okay." She smiled. The last week, John had been more focused and engaged than he had in a long time, and she was grateful. Yes, a lot of his focus had been him worrying over Leslie—rather, worrying that Nat would make him take care of Leslie on his own—but it was a start. John cooked and cleaned and ran errands and did just about anything she asked. Not that she wasn't frustrated that he still avoided any and all solo hands-on interactions with the baby, she was. But it was something. *Step-by-step.* She grinned. *Baby steps.* He wouldn't find that at all amusing. She tucked the mail under her arm and headed back to the porch.

John's uncertainty and fear was understandable, but…it was up to him to process and learn to cope with what was happening. It *was* happening. Leslie *wasn't* going anywhere. As much as she loved having them there, she couldn't pretend that John and Leslie were her whole life. They would leave, and when they left, she wanted a roof over her head and, hopefully, the Bear's House to run so the heartbreak wouldn't crush her. "It's just… the Bear's House is my place now. I have obligations, too…" And paying overtime, versus doing the work herself, wasn't sustainable.

"I respect that," he murmured, sounding uncertain.

She glanced at John, noting the deep pucker between his brows and her urge to smooth it. "I won't stay too long, but I have to make sure everything is running smoothly." She sighed, hating that she added, "Or I can call you, and if things are going to run late, you can bring Leslie up to the bar." But then folks would see him and know he was there.

Was that a bad thing? He'd been there for over a month now. Somewhere along the way, she'd gone from helping him to enabling him. It had to stop.

He ran a hand over his face. "We can't keep going like this."

She caught the front screen door before it could

slam, a lump forming in her throat. Hadn't she just been thinking the same thing? So why did hearing him say it trigger bone-deep fear? Her hands were shaking as she carried the mail into the kitchen and set it on the counter. "Like what?" she asked, looking at him.

"This." He was staring down at her, frowning now. "I know she's not your responsibility, Nat."

No, Leslie was *his* responsibility. But as he wasn't stepping up, what choice did Nat have? If John spent more time with Leslie, he'd see how dependent the baby was—for everything. Not that he didn't know that, he just didn't want to acknowledge it. For all the progress he'd been making—and the more upbeat attitude—he was still very good at skirting around things he didn't want to deal with. Like baby Leslie, his family and his knee…

She tore her gaze from his and started flipping through the mail, afraid her expression might give away what she was thinking.

A thin manila envelope caught her eye. It was more the handwriting, feminine and curly… And who it was addressed to. "John?" She held out the envelope, her stomach churning and a lump rising up to stick in her throat.

He didn't take it. Instead, all the color drained from his face, and he leaned against the counter. "Go ahead."

"It's addressed to you." She pressed it against

his chest. *This isn't my business.* Even if she had been caring for Leslie, around the clock, for the week… Leslie wasn't her baby. No matter how much she wished otherwise. *Stop.* Wanting things she couldn't have was never a good idea. Like John. And, now, Leslie… No, she needed to go open her intimidating packet and take care of *her* business. Preferably alone—so he wouldn't see her tears. "I'd be committing a felony if I opened your mail."

One eyebrow rose. "You know that, right off the top of your head?" He took the envelope. Instead of tearing it open, he set it down and stared at it.

"It's not a snake." She handed him the magnetic letter opener off the refrigerator, ignoring the shaking of her arm. "Not knowing won't make it go away." She was speaking to herself now, too. She had to stop avoiding what was happening. She had to take control before she had none and lost everything.

He glared at her, took the letter opener, slid it neatly across the envelope flap and handed the tool back to her. "There."

She stopped herself from snatching up the letter by reaching for the basket of dirty clothes and dropping her packet and the letter opener on top. "I'm going to get this in the wash while she's still asleep."

He nodded, still eyeing his envelope.

With a final glance, she carried the basket down the hall—taking care to avoid the squeaky board halfway—and flipped on the light in the utility room. She paused, taking a deep breath. Not that it helped. Her heart was still clipping along, and it hurt to breathe. She knew, deep down, she knew the letter was from Emily.

It could be a good thing. Maybe Emily had sent an address and a ticket or something, some way to get Leslie back to her.

Or not.

She swallowed and forced herself to put the soap in the washing machine, turn on the water and toss the load of baby onesies, blankets and a few of her formula-spattered shirts in. She closed the lid and leaned against it, trying to stop the surge of old insecurities and fears that had nothing to do with the here and now.

Emily had never been mean or abusive with Leslie. Leslie was a baby... Even if Emily had said horrible things to her daughter, Leslie wouldn't have understood. Like Nat, Leslie had been abandoned, but unlike Nat, Leslie had been left with caregivers—not left to fend for herself at the age of eight.

Leslie will never be in that situation.

It was an empty promise, really. Nat had no say over the baby. She wasn't family or a blood relation. She was Leslie's father's...what? Best friend?

Caretaker? Whatever she was, she had no input toward Leslie's fate. It didn't matter that, for the last week, Nat had been Leslie's everything—and vice versa. As much as she wished that precious baby girl belonged to her, she didn't. If Leslie was Nat's, she'd stop at nothing to keep that baby girl safe and happy. She'd love her, unconditionally, forever. *Like I already do.*

She shook her head and pressed her eyes shut, the baby monitor clipped to her waist playing the telltale sounds of Leslie stirring. *I wish you were mine, baby girl.* But the sad truth of it was no matter what happened now, Nat would have to make peace with the outcome—even if it ripped her heart out.

John sat on the front porch, gripping the manila envelope in his hands.

Emily had enclosed all of Leslie's original paperwork—her birth certificate, her shot record, her pediatrician's name and the signed adoption paperwork. She was signing away her rights to Leslie and leaving the rest up to John. *Because I know what the hell I'm doing.*

From his spot by the wicker rocking chair John had commandeered, Alpha rolled onto his back.

John absentmindedly rubbed the dog, his mind turning over Emily's note...

Vlad, watching John and Alpha from the safety of his hammock swing, made a click-chirp.

"What?" John asked. "You want something from me, too?"

Vlad showed his teeth and hissed.

"Right back at you," John snapped.

Alpha sat up, his head cocking to one side.

"Not you," he said, giving Alpha's ears a good scratching.

Alpha rested his chin on John's lap, his big brown eyes staring up at John—like he understood John needed someone to listen.

"I don't know what to do," he whispered. "I can't keep her…" But the second the words were out, his throat closed off. A hollow ache began in the pit of his stomach, and a sharp band of tension wrapped around his temples and down around the base of his skull.

Alpha blinked.

Adoption wasn't a bad thing. Leslie would have a family, a real family—with a father who wasn't…him. That's what he wanted, wasn't it? What the hell sort of father would he be? *Terrible, that's what*. He was more like his stepfather than his biological father. And his stepfather, he'd come to find out, was a lying, self-absorbed, mean-hearted son of a bitch who did a number on the once-strong bond between the Mitchell brothers. What was left of that bond? Well, his big brother, Hayden, had taken care of that. On him, constantly, to do more—to be more. Always there, questioning John's every thought and action, second-guessing him and doubting John's word.

Had John done his part? Hell, yes. If Hayden wasn't going to believe him, he might as well do what he was being accused of. Hayden had seemed too settled on John being a screwup, and John hadn't done a thing to correct him. It wouldn't have mattered anyway: once Hayden made up his mind about anything, it was a done deal. Hayden decided John was a lazy, worthless, no-good liar who never followed through or cared about anyone else. John decided to go with the path of least re-sistance and did his best to live up to every single one of his big brother's expectations.

From all he'd overheard at his last visit, Hayden's opinion of him hadn't changed.

What the hell did he know about being a fa-ther? Being responsible? Nurturing? He'd spent his whole life being the opposite of those things. *No.* Leslie would be better off without him.

And Nat?

He couldn't think about Nat. Not the way she hummed or rocked or patted or smiled at Leslie like she was the sun and the moon and the whole damn universe all rolled into one. If he did that… *No.*

"I'm not father material," he grumbled, forcing

the words out—needing to hear them. Assuming he *was* Leslie's father. No matter what the birth certificate read, there was a chance it was wrong.

Vlad clicked and chattered, like he was part of the conversation. There was no sign of his normal aggression, either. His ears were pricked forward, and his one beady eye fixed on John like he, too, was listening.

"Too bad I can't understand either of you. You and Alpha probably have it all figured out." John had to chuckle. Here he was, sitting on the front porch, dumping his troubles on a one-eyed raccoon and an arthritic Labrador.

"Or I could help." Nat's voice.

He turned to find her in the doorway, Leslie in her arms, watching him with those big blue eyes of hers. "She's up?" His banshee baby hadn't reached the same levels of hysteria since his mother had dropped off the baby monitor. Nat was really good at running interference and taking care of Leslie before things reached eardrum-shattering decibels.

"For a bit," Nat said. "I didn't want to interrupt the menfolk. The three of you seem to be having quite a conversation out here."

"Are we?" John's gaze traveled to the blanket-encased baby, the ache in his stomach spreading up, higher, into his chest.

"I'm guessing the letter isn't good news?" She

paused. "I mean, you're not acting like it's good news so..."

He couldn't stop staring at Leslie. *Was it good news? Or bad news?* "Hell, I don't know, Nat." He ran a hand over his face.

Nat pushed through the screen door, glanced back and forth between the raccoon-occupied swing and the rocker John was sitting in, and started walking back and forth—slowly—while bouncing Leslie. "It's from Emily?" she asked, glancing his way.

He nodded, his gaze falling to the manila envelope. "She's not coming back." Leslie was making an odd noise—one he'd never heard before. He stood and hurried to Nat. But it wasn't Leslie, it was Nat. "You okay?"

Nat nodded, but she wouldn't look at him.

"Nat?" he asked, his hands settling on her shoulders.

Still, she wouldn't look at him. "What did she say?" Her voice broke, and her indrawn breath was unsteady.

But now he was close and Leslie, tiny and squirming, was right here. The hollow ache was all over him now, hard and cold and horrible. "I think you know." He sounded gruff—a little angry.

Nat nodded. "What are you going to do?"

"I don't know." He sighed, his hold tightening on her. "We both know I'm not what's best for her."

Nat pulled away from him. "John…" She shook her head.

"What?" He hadn't meant to snap, but dammit, she knew he was right. "You've spent the last week taking care of her, not me. Because I can't take care of her—"

"Won't," Nat interrupted. "You *won't* take care of her."

John shook his head. "What do you want me to say, Nat? That one week and, poof, I'm ready to settle down and be a father? That Leslie here has turned me into a…a good man?" He swallowed. "We don't even know if she is mine."

She glanced at him, eyes narrowed. "Believe it or not, this has nothing to do with *you*, John." She was shaking, hard. "This is about your daughter. What is best for her?"

"That's what I'm talking about." He sighed. "I am not what's best for her."

"Fine. And your family? Your mother? What about them? You don't think they'd want to know about Leslie? That they might want to raise her?" She was staring up at him, her eyes glossy. "You think they'd be okay with you giving her up?"

"Now I need their approval?" It was a knee-jerk reaction. His instinct had always been to go on the defensive when it came to his family.

Nat was stunned speechless. But on her face… The disappointment…

Seeing her look at him like that hit as hard as a throat punch. "I... I—"

"You don't need anyone's approval." She sounded as disappointed as she looked. "Except your own. Whatever you decide, make sure you'll be able to look yourself in the eye. Make sure you've considered every possible option before you give her up, John. You have to. She's not a thing, John, she's your daughter."

"You've always given me the benefit of the doubt, Nat. Even when I don't deserve it. Like now." He ran a hand over his face. "I'm not the man you want me to be. I'm me. I can't change. I'll never be the sort of man that wakes up, realizing this is what I've been missing just because I played house with you for a week—sorry to disappoint you. That's not real life, Nat."

She stared up at him now, her eyes full of fight. "Playing house? If you think that's why I'm disappointed, you've got a rude awakening coming. I don't want this... Not any of it. I don't want a man who's more invested in finding ways to hold himself back than in moving forward. You think I want someone who doesn't see the good in anything? Someone who doesn't see what they have, right in front of them? Someone who lets their past eat away at whatever good could be in their future? I don't want that, John. I don't want you." She swallowed. "I did. For years, I did. I believed you were capable of anything. I lived for that smile of yours—waiting for that smile to be just for me. I loved you with my whole heart. But that smile and that John are gone." She shook her head. "I don't know who you are. The sad thing is I don't think you know who you are, anymore, either."

John couldn't think. Her words were on repeat. Horrible, wonderful, painful words. She loved him. *Past tense.* Now? *I don't want you.*

"I think it's best if you and Alpha and Leslie go." Her voice was shaking now.

"Go?" He could barely get the word out. She couldn't be serious? "Where the hell—"

"Home, John," she snapped. "Where you should have been this whole time. Where there are people who will love you and help you and support you and Leslie." She shook her head, a fat tear sliding out of the corner of her eye and down her cheek. "I love…love Leslie, and you're giving her up…"

That tear. The hurt in her voice. "Nat…"

"I mean it." She was staring at Leslie. "You're right. We can't do this anymore. The way you talk and act…about your daughter?" She drew in a wavering breath. "I need you to leave before there's nothing left to salvage of our friendship."

Nothing left? What the hell did that mean? "We'll go." He drew in a deep breath. He needed time to figure this out. He would. He'd figure out a way to make this better. "In the morning." When things were calm, she'd change her mind. She did love Leslie—

"Now, John." She turned. "I'll put Leslie in her car seat while you get your things, but it has to happen now."

He watched her go inside, heard the door slam, but he couldn't move. The pain in his heart was damn near crippling. He didn't want Nat to think of him this way. He didn't want her to send him away—disappointed and angry. For now, there wasn't much he could do... She wanted him gone. She'd made that perfectly clear. With Leslie in tow, there was only one place he *could* go.

He headed inside, picked up the phone and dialed home.

"Hello?" his mother answered on the first ring.

"Mom, it's John." He cleared his throat. "I'm home."

"You are?" She sounded so damn happy. "Where are you?"

He ran a hand over his face. "I'm at Nat's place." There was silence. "I was hoping you'd bring the truck over. For all the baby stuff. Leslie... Leslie, the baby? She's my daughter." He'd never thought the words, let alone said them out loud. But, somehow, saying them made them...real.

"I'm on my way, John," his mother said, not hesitating. "I love you."

He pressed his eyes shut and leaned against the

porch railing. "I love you, too, Mom." He hung up, wishing he could go back in time and make the right decisions this time. All of them. His stepfather. Fighting with Hayden. His disregard for authority. His insubordination…

But there was so much more. How had he been so blind? So stubborn? Never knowing, never seeing, that he had the love of the only woman who was ever worthy of loving. He was one lucky son of a bitch. At every turn, he'd taken her for granted. Expecting her to be there for him or come running when he needed her. He was a damn fool—for years—but lucky. Until now, he hadn't realized just how much. He had Nat.

She was right. He didn't know who he was, not anymore. But he better figure it out, and quick, because the only thing he did know? He loved Natalie Harris, and he was going to do whatever it took to try to win her love back.

Chapter Nine

Nat changed Leslie's diaper, put her in a clean onesie and lay her in the crib. "You're going to meet your family." She stroked the downy softness of the infant's cheek. "And you are going to be so loved, little one." There was no doubt about that. "Let me pack up a few things."

Leslie yawned.

Nat ignored the sting in her eyes and turned, focusing on the task at hand. Packing. She rubbed her hands against her thighs, but it didn't stop them from trembling. This was the right thing, she knew it was, but it didn't make it any easier.

She pulled one of the empty boxes from the closet, crouched by the changing table and started transferring the few blankets, clothes and odds and ends from the drawers into the box. She added the toys Jan had brought and the plastic baby bath before sitting back and looking around. Without the crib and changing table, there would be no sign that Leslie had ever been here. The thought sliced through her chest, turning the sting in her eyes to an outright burn.

"Looks like you got everything." John's voice was low and gruff.

She didn't look at him; she couldn't.

"I called. Mom should be bringing the truck so we can get all of this." He cleared his throat. "No need to go back and forth."

She managed a nod.

Alpha trotted in and sat beside her.

"Don't forget his dog food." She gave the dog a scratch behind the ear.

"Figured I'd leave some for Vlad."

Vlad would appreciate that. He loved Alpha's food.

"She's clean." Nat stood, nodding at the crib. "I'll put her into her car seat when you're ready to go. No point in getting her worked up until then."

"The longer we can delay her banshee wail, the better."

He was trying to tease, to be playful, and it made the pain in her heart ten times worse. She brushed past him, refusing to cry one more tear in his presence. Instead, she hurried to her bathroom, closed the door and washed her face with ice-cold water. *Be strong.* She stared at her reflection. As much as she wanted them to stay, she knew she wasn't doing any of them any favors. John had been right: this wasn't real life. And the longer they were here, the harder the return to reality would be.

"I have things to do," she told her reflection. "A business and home to save." People were counting on her. The Bear's House didn't run itself. If it closed, good people would be out of work. "I can't let that happen."

John needed to sort his life out.

She needed to sort her life out.

After that... "I guess we'll see."

She was relieved to hear the slam of a truck door. Then another. Jan wasn't alone?

For all her insistence to stay out of John's business, she found herself drying her hands and hurrying out to greet whichever Mitchells had shown up to help.

Leslie and Alpha were still in the nursery, so Nat scooped up the baby and carried her down the hall into the front room. She didn't know who or what sort of reception she was going to get. After all, she had lied to Jan... About everything.

"Nat." Kyle Mitchell nodded. "Good to see you."

"You, too." She managed what she hoped was a smile and shifted Leslie in her arms.

"This is my niece?" Kyle asked, stepping forward to peer down at Leslie. "She's a tiny little thing, isn't she?" He shook his head and stepped back. "Sorta glad Greer came in a larger size. Not sure I'd know how to handle something so small."

"You'd learn." Jan Mitchell slipped an arm around Nat's waist. "Thank you, Nat. For taking such good care of Leslie. And, I suspect, John, too."

"Leslie was easy." Nat turned, glancing at John. Kyle chuckled.

"No arguing that." John stood off to one side, the box from Leslie's room under one arm. "Nat's a saint. Always has been. Putting up with all my sh—"

"John Henry," Jan cut him off. "There will be none of that language, you hear me?"

"I hear you." The corner of John's mouth cocked up. "Sorry."

"You don't want her washing your mouth out with soap," Kyle murmured. "She will, too."

"Guess some things never change." John's gaze swiveled and locked with Nat's.

For a minute, Nat was thrown. What did that look mean? *No.* It didn't matter. He could be as charming as he wanted, but he was leaving. Nat needed some space and time away from John to get over feeling things she'd thought she'd let go of years before.

"How are things over at the Bear's House?" Kyle asked.

"Good." She patted Leslie's back. If there were no tax troubles, it would be more than good. But she wasn't about to unload that here and now.

"I'm sure they are." Jan's arm stayed around

her waist. "You've always been a force of nature, Natalie. Strong and steady, no matter what life throws your way." She chuckled. "Including John."

"I'd say he's the force of nature," Nat argued.

"Nat's always been the calm in the storm." John's voice was unusually soft. "More like a lighthouse."

Nat wasn't sure what to say to that. From the looks of it, Jan and Kyle were a little thrown, too. But Leslie chose that moment to start wiggling and grunting, effectively shifting the focus of the room. Alpha, knowing the drill, trotted to the front door. "I've put all her paperwork and notes and… everything in the diaper bag," she murmured, taking a deep breath and offering the baby to Jan. "I'm sure you'll be just fine. Be good, little Leslie."

Jan eased Leslie into her arms, giving Nat a long, assessing look. "You come and see her whenever you want." She paused. "How about you come on over for dinner tonight? We've been trying for ages—"

"I have to work," Nat cut her off. "But maybe later on. After things are…worked out." She didn't elaborate.

"The offer is good, whenever you're free." Jan smiled, patting Leslie's back.

"I'll get her car seat strapped in," Nat murmured.

"I can get it." Kyle grabbed the handle. "I'm a pro

at car seats." He also managed to carry out Leslie's diaper bag and a box.

Jan gave her a one-armed hug, holding Leslie close with the other. "We will see you real soon."

Nat nodded, her gaze fixed on the top of Leslie's head. "Yes, ma'am." But her voice wobbled, and her eyes were stinging again. She watched as Jan carried Leslie from the house and out under the bright Texas sun. With each step, Nat felt something inside draw tight around her lungs.

"You going to be okay?" John's hand rested on her shoulder.

She nodded, avoiding his gaze. "Fine. Back to normal." Alone. *Me and Vlad and the IRS letters.* Her lungs continued to deflate while a hollowness settled in the base of her stomach.

"Nat." His voice was low and gruff.

"No, John." She brushed his hand from her shoulder. "We've said enough today. Let's just… leave it. You need to get Leslie home before she gets too hungry. And you've got your doctor's appointment, don't forget."

"I won't." His light brown eyes swept over her face. "I'll let you know."

"You don't have to. It's none of my business." She stepped back, shrugging. "Take care of yourself, John. I'm sure I'll see you around."

He stood there so long, Nat worried he'd say something that would trigger the tears she was working so hard to hold back. Finally, he nodded. "You will." He tucked the hair behind her ear and headed for the door.

Nat stood on the porch and watched, holding her tears at bay until they were gone. Then she collapsed into Grampa Bear's rocking chair and sobbed, Vlad crawling into the hammock swing to watch her with his one good eye.

John parked the Jeep, put his cowboy hat on and helped Alpha down from the Jeep. "Here's hoping this goes better this time around." He gave Alpha a scratch behind the ear.

Kyle had barely parked before his mother was out, unbuckling a wailing Leslie from the back seat and holding her close.

"Banshee Baby," he murmured.

"I guess she's hungry." His mother offered him the baby. "I'll get a bottle made up."

"I can make the bottle." He stared at the baby. "You can…bond with her." He'd rather have a few minutes before he revealed just how inept he was when it came to the whole parenting thing.

His mother beamed. "If you're sure you don't mind." She smiled down at Leslie. "I'd love to get to know you, sweet little angel."

"Good one," Kyle murmured. "Using the *bonding* card." He chuckled. "There's also *needing some Gramma time*. That one gets her every time."

John grabbed the diaper bag from the rear of the Jeep. "It's true. But thanks for the tip." He sighed, confessing, "Plus, I'm scared I'll drop her."

"Yeah, I get that." Kyle followed them inside. "Greer is like two times Leslie's size, and I still worry about that." He clapped John on the shoulder.

"Good to know." John wasn't so sure about that. He'd hoped his fear of holding Leslie would fade. *Guess not.* He didn't pause; he headed straight into the kitchen and pulled out everything for a bottle. He had the steps down: it was one of the few baby things he'd mastered.

"She is the sweetest little thing." His mother cradled Leslie in her arms, rocking slowly in their grandmother's rocking chair. Leslie's fusses were mounting.

"She's little, all right." He tested the temperature on his wrist. "But she has lungs. I call her Banshee Baby. Nat doesn't like it."

"Things all right?" his mother asked. "Between the two of you?"

He heard Kyle's chuckle but decided to shrug it off. "Fine." But a shadow on the back porch caught his eye, and his throat went dry and tight.

"Momma," Hayden said, walking in the back door. "You look happy." He crossed to the rocking chair and stared down at Leslie. "Tiny." He glanced his way. "John."

"Hayden," he murmured, carrying the bottle to his mother. No matter what, he was going to keep his cool. He had to. Between Leslie and Emily and Nat, sticking it out in Granite Falls was his only option.

"Been a while since I've had all my boys under one roof." She took the bottle, her gaze bouncing from Hayden to Kyle to him. "And now, here you are." She smiled down at Leslie. "These fine strapping men are your uncles, Leslie."

"I'm getting the feeling she's not all that impressed." Kyle chuckled.

"Leave the little angel alone," their mother chided. "She's hungry from all the growing she's doing."

"I'd be okay with her growing a little faster." John still wasn't convinced it was healthy for her to be this small. It was one of the things he'd talk to the doctor about today.

"Mark my words, you'll be wanting time to slow down before too long." His mother kept right on rocking. "I can remember when you three were this size. Like it was yesterday. There are times I think babies are the easiest part of parenting."

Between Kyle and his mother, they weren't selling John on the whole parenting thing.

"Toddlerhood is a barrel of *no*s and tears. Then school starts, and there's all the *who is friends with who* and making good grades and sports. High school comes along, and testosterone and competition kicks in, and hold on to your hats." She spoke softly, crooning the whole time. "Once your little ones get to be adults, there's not much you can do but stand back and watch and hope they come through all right. *Unless* you see one of your babies heading for trouble." She paused. "And, boys, I see that. Here and now, between you, Hayden, and you, John. I can't make you hug it out like I used to, but I'm going to speak my peace, and I expect you both to listen."

"Yes, ma'am." He and Hayden spoke in unison.

"You are family. You will be until the day you die." She looked up at them. "You're both so hard-headed, so proud, I fear that'll stop the two of you from ever truly being brothers. You hear me?"

John heard her all right. "I hear you."

"And you?" she asked Hayden.

"Yes, ma'am." Hayden nodded, the muscle in his jaw working.

"You boys are all fathers now, starting families and back home in Granite Falls." She went back to cooing over Leslie. "I'd say you've been given a second chance."

John risked a glance Hayden's way.

Hayden was staring at the floor, his hands on his hips.

"I'll stop now." His mother stood. "I think this

little miss angel here needs a burp and a diaper. You can give me a hand, John?"

He glanced at the clock, not wanting to be late for the doctor's appointment.

"Going somewhere?" Hayden asked, his tone curt.

"Are you leaving?"

The look of heartbreak on their mother's face had John offering up a quick explanation. "Just a doctor's appointment." He nodded at Leslie. "Checkup is all. They squeezed us in."

"But you'll be back for supper?" His mother had a way of asking a question that sounded more like an order.

He nodded, following her down the hall to what had once been a guest room.

"Weston's room." She smiled, pointing out the stenciled cowboy hats and horseshoe trim that bordered the room. "I wanted a minute, John." She swallowed, searching his face. "When I dropped by Nat's, before I knew Leslie was yours, she'd mentioned something about the father being uncertain." She paused. "Are you? Uncertain?"

John blew out a long, slow breath. "Mom, I'm still figuring out which way is up."

"I'll take that as a yes." His mother glanced down at Leslie.

"I don't even know if she's mine, Mom." His cheeks felt hot. "Today, the doctor… I'm finding out."

His mother was watching him. "She looks just like you did, John. Just like you." She offered Leslie. "Take her a minute, so I can get a diaper."

"I can get it." But his mother placed a hand on his arm, stopping him.

"I'll get it." She carefully slid Leslie into his arms. "You wait here."

John froze, too scared to breathe, let alone move. All he could do was hold on to the wriggling bundle in his arms. The bundle that squeaked.

"You're good." *I'm not.* "You're fine." He winced at Leslie's squeak. "She thinks she's being clever. Your…gramma, I mean. She thinks leaving us alone will change things." He sighed.

Leslie squirmed, bunched up and belched loudly before smiling. Nat had told him she was too young to smile; it was more gas bubbles.

"Gas bubbles or not, that was something." John chuckled.

It was the first time he'd been alone with Leslie. He moved, slowly, to the rocking chair in the corner and sat, resting Leslie against his thighs so he could look at her. Nat said she was pretty, like a little doll. His mother called her a little angel. "When you're not screaming bloody murder, you're cute." He grinned when her little fist popped free of the blanket. He reached for it, watching her tiny hand clasp on to one of his fingers. "First Nat, then my mom. It's like they think I'm going to get struck by some sort of lightning and, all of a sudden, I'll be some sort of super dad." Leslie grunted and wriggled again. "Like that's going to happen." Even if he wanted to try this whole fatherhood thing, he'd be doing Leslie a disservice. "Take it from me, Leslie, I'd only screw things up." He ran his thumb over her fingers, still wrapped around his finger. "And that's not right. I'm going to do my best, here, kid." He swallowed. "To give you the best."

Nat was right: it was a huge decision. And this time, he needed to pick what was right over what he may or may not want. It would be a whole hell of a lot easier if he knew what he wanted.

Chapter Ten

Nat took the stockroom-inventory list from Walt. "Thanks."

"You look beat," Walt, who rarely spoke more than one word at a time, said. "What's up?"

Nat shook her head. "I have a lot on my plate, that's all." *And I'm not sleeping.* She decided not to share that with him.

"IRS thing?" he asked.

She nodded. "I'm hoping the motorcycle sales will make a huge difference." She'd reached out to Harry James, one of Grampa Bear's old buddies and a motorcycle collector, about what she could make if she put Grampa Bear's bikes up for auction. There was no reason for her to hang on to seven motorcycles, she knew that, but it didn't make it any easier. Each of the bikes had been significant to her grandfather—meaning they were significant to her.

I'm sorry, Grampa. It's not like I have much of a choice. She pinched the bridge of her nose, willing the constant ache to dissipate.

"You sure you're okay?" Walt asked, his usual gruffness tempered with genuine concern.

Nat looked at the man. He was six-five, had tattooed sleeves down both arms, a pierced ear, a jagged scar through his right eyebrow and was missing his left pinkie from a motorcycle accident. Walt had lived a hard life. Thanks to Grampa Bear, he'd kicked his drug addiction and gone to night school to get his GED. He was now close to graduating from his online university with a finance and business degree. "I will be." She smiled at him.

"Nat…" Walt broke off. "I've been thinking." He shrugged. "You could sell the place."

"I can't." She shook her head. "This place was everything to him—"

"Not everything." Walt sighed. "You were, though. He'd worry about you now."

Nat ignored the stinging in her eyes. "No need." She forced a smile. "I'm tough. Just like he taught me to be." She had the feeling Walt had more to say, but the ringing of the telephone cut things short. It was a relief. It'd been four days since John and Leslie had left her place, and she'd been walking an emotional tightrope ever since.

When she was at work, she was wondering what was happening with Leslie and John.

When she was at home, she was wondering that same thing. Worse, she'd finally manage to doze off then jerk awake thinking she'd heard Leslie.

Mostly, she missed them.

It didn't seem to matter that Leslie had only been with her a week. Nat ached something fierce for the baby girl. As tempted as she'd been to call and check in, she knew going cold turkey was the best thing for her. Not that it stopped John from calling daily and leaving a detailed message about Leslie. Lucky for her, he called when she was working or she'd have answered the phone by now.

As it was, she was haunted by the way they'd parted. She'd said too much. Admitting she loved him? Why had she done that? What possible good could come from telling him? Of course, she'd told a teeny white lie, saying she had been in love with him... Not that she *was* in love with him. So that was something, she supposed.

Still, she'd managed not to sob her way through buckling Leslie into her car seat, waiting, instead, for Jan's truck to pull away, before falling apart. Instead of wallowing, she'd showered, dressed and left the house to climb into Grampa Bear's old beat-up truck and head straight to the Bear's House. She'd stayed late and fallen face-first into her bed when she returned home, well after closing hours.

It had become a routine of sorts. Get up, have coffee with Vlad, get dressed, go to the Bear's House and head home in the wee hours of the morning. She was running on fumes but that was good. If she was worn out, she didn't have time to linger over her broken heart.

"Bachelor party," Walt said, nodding at the group of men coming through the front door.

She frowned, giving Walt a look. The Bear's House was pretty old-school. One large-screen television permanently tuned in to whatever sport was currently playing. A few pool tables, a poker table, darts, an ancient and finicky jukebox, bikers of all ages and every kind of alcohol. The Watering Hole, in town, was the trendy place to go. All sorts of televisions and a dance floor, theme nights, fancy-named drink specials and a wall covered in flashy neon lights. It was no surprise that the Watering Hole saw far more bachelor parties than the Bear's House.

But then Nat caught sight of Buzz Lafferty, all smiles, and waved. "What are you doing here?" she asked.

"Figured we'd slum it tonight." Buzz winked. "How's it going?"

Buzz Lafferty had been a staple in many of her childhood adventures. He was all respectable now, the town veterinarian and owner of Granite Falls Veterinary Clinic and Hospital. He was still cheeky and outspoken and more flirtatious than any other man in town, but Nat was glad to call him a friend. "With you here? It's bound to get all sorts of interesting now."

"You look good," he said, resting his elbows on the bar.

"Thank you." She rolled her eyes. "How's life?"

"Decent. Of course, it's always a day of mourning when a buddy gives up the good life and ties the knot, but I figure there's not much I can do about it." He shrugged.

"Guess not." Nat laughed. "Who are we mourning tonight?" She'd been so out of the loop, she hadn't caught wind of any new engagements. Her gaze searched the group of cowboy-hat-wearing individuals taking up residence at the tables by the dartboards.

"Mr. Kyle Mitchell, of course." Buzz shook his head. "I like Skylar and all, she is the best damn veterinary technician I've ever had, but… I don't see why he has to up and marry her."

At the mention of Kyle's name, she felt a twinge of panic. If Kyle was here, so were the other Mitchell brothers. *It's their brother's bachelor party…* But if John was here, was she really up to staying?

"I mean, why get married?" Buzz went on, grimacing.

"I hear some people like married life." She shrugged. She'd enjoyed *playing house* with John and Leslie…even if it had been pretending.

"Not me." Buzz winked at her. "How about you

and I make a pact, right here and now, never to get married."

"I'm okay with that." She winked right back. "Buzz Lafferty, I will never marry you."

Buzz burst out laughing.

"Drink?" she asked once he'd quieted down.

"I'm here to get four pitchers of beer." He nodded, tipping his cowboy hat back. "And a round of shots, too."

She filled pitchers, then shot glasses, her gaze sweeping the dimly lit interior in the hopes that Walt would step up and help Buzz with the drinks. She wasn't exactly hiding from John… *I'm totally hiding.* Why test her limits? There was no need. Lucky for her, Walt emerged from the stockroom just about the time she'd finished pouring all the shot glasses.

"Can you take this?" she asked.

"Okay." The great thing about Walt, his face rarely gave anything away. He hefted the tray and followed Buzz, who carried a pitcher in each hand, to the back corner of the Bear's House, but she decided the best way to get through the rest of the evening was to pretend this was any other night— that no one special was here.

After she'd cleaned off tables, made two trips to the stockroom and managed to eat half a brisket sandwich before her nerves got the better of her, she began to think about heading home. But tonight, every slide of the chair legs on the floor or the thump of boots on board heading her way had her breaking out into a cold sweat. She was jumpy, and even though Walt hadn't said a thing, she could tell it was making him jumpy, too.

"You think you can handle things?" she asked Walt a few minutes after midnight.

"Yep." He nodded, giving her the side-eye. "Go on home."

"I think I will." She tugged off her apron, hung it on the hook on the back wall and collected her purse. "See you later." Some people might consider her behavior cowardly. She preferred to think of it as self-preservation.

"'Night," Walt murmured.

She waved, trying not to run—the flight instinct bubbling up with each step closer to the door. She was almost there, almost home free, when she heard John call out her name. Instead of acknowledging him, she moved faster. If she pretended she couldn't hear him—

"I know you heard me, Nat," he said. "You jumped a good ten feet when I said your name."

Which was a total exaggeration. Or, at least, a slight exaggeration. Her heart was racing, and her stomach was in knots, but she had to say something. With her hand on the door, she murmured, "Heading home." *Don't turn around.* "Tell Kyle congratulations for me. And have fun. Walt will take care of you." She pushed the door open and stepped outside, pausing to suck air from her achingly empty lungs.

The sky overhead was deep blue but too hazy to see much of the millions of stars that usually lit her walk. Normally, she loved the quiet amble home. It helped her shift gears from work mode to home mode. But tonight, she wished she had Bear's truck. It was old and noisy, but it would have gotten her to her house and away from John that much faster. The faster, the better.

John stared at the door. He should have let her be. It was clear she didn't want to have anything to do with him. He'd tried. All night, he'd tried. But every second of every minute of every hour they'd been there, he'd known exactly where Nat was and what she was doing. When he'd been throwing darts, she'd been talking to Buzz. When he'd been listening to Angus and Dougal McCarrick regale him with their latest victories on the cutting-horse circuit, she'd been cleaning off tables. And when he'd been losing his ass at pool to his brothers, she'd been sliding glasses into the rack over the bar. She must have been on a step stool, and every time she reached up, the hem of her shirt rose, exposing the creamy skin and belly button beneath. He'd damn near hit the ball off the table when she'd bent forward, giving him an all too tantalizing peek down the front of her skintight Bear's House shirt.

If he'd gotten short and snippy, he couldn't help it. Tonight was supposed to be about Kyle. Cutting loose and having fun. Getting out and away and forgetting…everything. Instead, he'd been forced to endure all the wanting and aching and tightening of the viselike hold on his heart each and every time he caught a glimpse of Nat.

"What's up?" Buzz Lafferty asked. "Have you suddenly developed an interest in doors? 'Cuz you're sure giving that one a thorough inspection."

John ran a hand over his face. Buzz had sarcasm down to an art form. Sometimes it was more enjoyable than others… Now was not one of those times.

"So…" Buzz cleared his throat. "You've been eyeing her all night." He held up a hand. "No point denying it. We all noticed." Hands on hips, he gave John an assessing look. "Something going on with you two?"

John shook his head. "Nothing." *Because I'm a damn fool.*

"You piss her off?" he asked. "She did sort of run out of here."

John didn't bother holding back his glare now.

"I'll take that as a yes." Buzz sighed. "You always were good at pissing people off, John. You used to be just as good at charming them, too. So what the hell happened?"

He kept right on glaring.

Buzz wasn't the least big fazed by John's glare. If he had been, he wouldn't have kept speaking. "This is Nat we're talking about. She's always been your biggest supporter. I can't help but think that's why you had been hiding out at her place for so long. You know she'd always get your back." He paused. "Whatever you did, fix it. Fix it or you'll regret it."

John didn't want to have this conversation with Buzz. Not here, not now... *Not ever.* It didn't matter that Buzz was right—that he needed to fix it. If he could, he would. But he didn't know how. Or where to start. *He'd screwed up, big-time. Again.*

"I'm taking a walk," John mumbled, pushing out the front door. Instead of wandering, he set off with a purpose. His feet knew where he was going even if his brain refused to accept it. His pace was brisk, straining his knee but not slowing him.

He could see her, strolling along—taking her sweet time. If she knew he was following her, would she take off running? But now that he'd admitted he was following her, it felt wrong. He didn't want to trap her or surprise her. He wanted...he wanted...

"Nat?" he called out, noting her stumble. "Hey."

She wasn't moving now. "John?"

Yeah, it's me. His decision to trail after her, in the dark, probably hadn't been his best idea. She knew he wasn't some creepy guy… At least, he hoped so. "I figured I'd walk you home."

"I'm fine." There was a snap to her tone. "Thank you."

He sighed, all the frustration he'd been struggling with the last four days grabbing him by the throat. Words, so many words, vied to come first. What he did say took him by surprise. "You're fine? That makes one of us."

Nat started walking again, Bear's front-porch light a beacon in the mostly darkened street. "John…" She shook her head, her pace quickening. "I don't think there's much left to say."

"Maybe there are a few things I need to say." *A few things?*

"Can they wait? I'm tired." She sounded exhausted. No, worse, she sounded defeated.

He almost turned back, almost. "No."

It was too dark to see her face, but he could tell she glanced over her shoulder, looking his way. She didn't say anything until they were walking up the steps to her porch. "Go on," she said, crossing her arms over her chest and staring up at him. The tilt of her head was pure defiance. She was so damn beautiful.

He gave himself a minute to take her in—he'd missed looking at her. She appeared exhausted. Bone-tired. What could he do to make her smile? To take some of the starch out of her and soften her just the slightest bit? "Leslie is good. And she's mine."

Her gaze fell from his.

"Mom is in love with her." He swallowed. "You were right about that, too."

Nat hugged herself, her gaze fixed on the porch at her feet.

"I just wanted you to know that." He swallowed again.

"You could have said all that in a message."

I wanted to see you. "I guess I could have." He sighed. "I'm… I'm sorry, too."

Her gaze met his then. "For?"

"Where should I start?" He smiled. She was looking at him now. That was something. "All of it. For putting you in that position. I know how you feel about honesty, and I made you lie, for me, to everyone." He fought against that damnable urge to reach for her.

She nodded. "Thank you."

"I—I miss you, Nat." More than he could ever have expected.

She didn't say anything or do anything, but those big blue eyes of hers stayed locked with his.

"I guess I was hoping, maybe, you missed me a little, too?" He knew he sounded pathetic, but dammit, it was true. While he was spending hours worrying over her, was she thinking of him?

"You said it, John. We were *playing house*…"

She shrugged. "Playing. Not real. You can't miss something that wasn't real. Not really."

He didn't like her answer. Not one damn bit. "*You* are real." He stepped closer to her, giving up the fight. He didn't want space between them, not anymore.

"I am." Her voice was high and tight. "I'm a real *person*. Not just a caretaker or a crutch or a pal. I'm a woman——"

"I know it." His hand hovered by her cheek, looking for any sign of resistance. "A woman I can't stop reaching for." His fingers trailed along the curve of her cheek. Finally, finally, he was touching her. "Thinking about." He stepped closer still, the telltale shudder of her shirt front and the rasp of her breath stoking a fire in his blood. "Wanting." He was almost growling now. "I can't stop wanting you."

Nat opened her mouth, but nothing came out. Instead, she did the last thing he'd expected. She grabbed the front of his shirt, rose up on tiptoe and kissed him. It was soft, tentative—almost testing. But it did something to them both, flipped some sort of switch and opened the floodgates.

He felt it in her, the sudden intensity in her grip and the way she arched—straining against him.

One minute his touch was featherlight against her cheek, the next he was cupping the back of her head and exploring the fullness of her mouth. Soft lips. Firm. Parting beneath his. Sweet breath, mixing with his. The touch of her silky tongue and the shudder that touch caused.

His hands couldn't get enough of her. Stroking and cupping, kneading and sliding over each and every delectable curve. This was Nat. His Nat. She was the one who set his blood on fire and rocked his world. She was the one twining her arms around his neck and gasping against his lips. This was all he wanted, right here. Nat.

She is right where she is meant to be.

"I missed you," he said, dropping kisses along her neck. He'd dreamed this. Kissing her this way. He'd imagined the way she'd taste, the way she'd feel…but he hadn't come close. Nothing had prepared him for the surge of feelings pulling him under. It wasn't just wanting, it was so much more—

"John." Nat's voice was husky.

He was exploring the curve of her neck with his nose, making his way up to her ear, but he paused. That was when he noticed the low growl coming from the corner of the porch. He raised his head, his eyes narrowing to search the dark. There it was. A large, hulking shadow, one beady eye fixed on him. *Vlad.* "This has nothing to do with you," he argued, chuckling in spite of himself.

"He's been a little more protective since you and Alpha left," Nat said, drawing in a deep breath.

"Good raccoon," John said. "Now, shoo."

Nat laughed. "It's his porch." Her blue eyes fell to his lips. "You could…come inside?"

"Are you sure?" he asked, torn between saying good-night and staying.

She nodded.

"You're sure?" he repeated, unable to stop himself from running his thumb along her lower lip.

She nodded again. "Wouldn't want Vlad to attack you."

"Fair point." He took the hand she offered and followed her into house.

Chapter Eleven

Nat was pretty sure this was all a dream. All of it. She'd invited him in—when she should have said good-night. And as soon as the door closed behind them and he'd kicked it shut, what had she done? Launched herself at him. Without hesitation. She'd kissed him. Was still kissing him. She was kissing John? It couldn't be happening.

"Nat." He sounded gruff and velvety and toe-curlingly desperate. His nose brushed behind her ear.

She'd promised herself she'd never do such a thing. Kiss John, that is. *Like this.*

The warmth of his breath fanned across her skin and stirred her hair. Her hands twined around his waist, needing support. But the doubt was there. He needed help. Was this…about Leslie…? He needed help with Leslie… His lips sucked her earlobe into his mouth. Her head fell back, a delicious wave of molten heat rolling over her. John… This…

His hand rested on her rib cage, right beneath the swell of her breast. His mouth caught hers, clinging and persistent and erasing all reason and thought and resistance.

How long had she wanted John Mitchell? Was there a time she hadn't wanted him? If there was, she couldn't remember it. And now…why resist? Why deprive herself of something she had *always* wanted? *Because…*

"Dammit, Nat," he said, against her lips. "You feel so good." His hand slid up enough to cup her breast.

Speaking wasn't possible. Not when his thumb traced across her nipple or when his mouth sealed to hers once more. If she could speak, she knew exactly what she'd say. *Please don't stop.*

His hand slid under her shirt, pushing up the fabric just high enough that he could stoop and explore her lace-covered breast with his mouth. She was groaning then, arching off the door, tugging at his shirt—all the while blissfully focused on the sensation of his tongue and teeth against the supersensitive tip of her barely covered breast.

She shrugged out of her shirt, ignoring the warning tingle in her stomach.

His fingers were rough, teasing her nerves, as he brushed the sensitive skin between her breasts…and found the clasp there.

She'd never be considered a small woman. Her curves were who she was, but now…there was something almost reverent in the way John touched her. He wasn't rushed or aggressive. He was deliberate and intent. He nuzzled and kissed, sucked and licked until Nat was on the verge of coming apart at the seams.

Her hold on his shirt had tightened and tightened to the point that tugging it off took very little effort. Then they were skin-to-skin. His muscles and scars against her soft roundness. It was a shock to the system—this sudden intimacy—one that had her staring up at him. He was waiting.

That was when the hard truth slammed into her. This wasn't right. *This can't happen.* "John…" She was panting, the enormity of what was happening between them collapsing her chest in on itself.

The passion on his face was a thing of beauty. He wanted her. He was shaking with want for her. And her blood was humming with hunger for him. But…

"This—" she sucked in a deep breath "—this can't happen." She took another breath. "We will both regret it."

He shook his head. "How the hell could I regret this?" His hands slid down her bare back, sending a shudder along her spine.

"Because it will ruin our friendship." The words were harsh but necessary.

John's brows pulled together, his lips turning down. "It doesn't have to."

"But it will." She hurried on, needing to convince herself that this was all wrong. "You'll never see me the same way, and I'll always wonder why this happened...now."

"Nat—"

"No. Don't. We both know you can talk me into this. I'm asking you not to." She stepped back, crossing her arms over her bare chest. "I can't separate this from my heart. For me, this means something, and we... This can't happen." Because her heart couldn't take it.

"You know I care about you," he murmured, his gaze searching hers. "I mean I... I—"

"Stop. Stop there." She shook her head. If he pushed, turned on the charm, pleaded just a little, she'd cave. She'd fall into bed and pretend that he wasn't looking for a person and place to take care of him and Leslie, that this was about him wanting *her.* "I know you care about me, John. But that's not what I'm talking about. If we did this, I'd be deceiving myself—because..." *I want to believe you love me.* He didn't, of course, not the way she wanted. And if he said he did, now? He'd be fooling himself, too—saying what he needed to say to get what he wanted. "Let's say good-night and... forget this ever happened."

"If you think I can forget this—"

"I know you can." She grabbed her bra and slid it on, fastening the clasp and avoiding eye contact.

"What does that mean?" His words were gruff and clipped.

"You forgot about Emily. Your weekend to-gether." She turned, searching for her shirt. "You can forget about this." A jagged lump hung in her throat, and her eyes stung.

John didn't say a word.

Silence. Absolute silence. The longer it went on, the harder it was not to look at him. *That would be a mistake.* Everything she was saying was true. Harsh, but true. And yet, she didn't want to hurt him—she loved him. But that didn't mean she was okay with him using her as his personal doormat. Her gaze met his. *Big mistake.*

He reached for her, anguished. "Nat, this is not the same thing."

She dodged his hand. "I know." She swallowed, her gaze holding his. "This is worse. I'm not some nameless, faceless woman you don't ever have to worry about looking in the eye again."

His hand fell.

"What happens tomorrow?" She shook her head, more than a little distracted by his shirtless status. "What is the goal here? You and Leslie move back in, and we go back to playing house? Or is this just another one-night stand?" She paused, watching the shift of emotions on his face. "You don't know, do you? But you're still willing to risk our friendship for this? For sex?"

He was staring at her, his expression guarded. "I'm not."

She welcomed the first flare of anger. "You've been my best friend—always. One of the few constants in my life. But…I'm beginning to think our friendship doesn't mean the same thing to you. Do you even like me, John? Or do you keep me around because, every once in a while, I'm useful?"

John stepped back, the muscles in his jaw working.

Maybe she'd crossed the line. Did she really doubt that John was her friend? No. She was upset. But lashing out wouldn't help things.

She swallowed, hard. If she didn't stand her ground now, she'd hate herself—all over again. Since he'd left, she'd had a lot of time to think about the precedent she'd set. He wasn't fully to blame for taking advantage of her. She could have spoken up instead of staying quiet, but she'd been too worried about upsetting John. Instead of worrying over upsetting him, she should have thought about what was best for him. Not indulging him with an endless supply of beer, cable, a comfy couch and zero accountability for anything.

"Is that really what you think?" There was a hardness to him now. "That I'm using you?"

"I think you don't know what you want. And I think Leslie and your injury and your uncertain future has made you question everything." She shrugged. "Including my role in your life—if I have one."

"Of course you have one." He ran a hand over his face. "I mean, I hope you… Damn, Nat, what do you want? What are you saying?"

"You need to figure things out. Get your stuff straight. Know what you want. You have to grow up, John. Like it or not, you have responsibilities— the kind that won't go away." She bent, grabbed her shirt off the floor and straightened, pulling it over her head. "Then we can talk about us. Whatever *us* means."

He took her hand, the lost expression on his face tugging at her heart. "I can't see you until then?"

"I'm not saying that…" What was she saying? She stared down at their joined hands. "I just think, after tonight… Things are a little mixed up. Maybe taking a break will—"

"Make me stop wanting you?" he asked. "It's not like I can flip a switch, Nat."

His words were like an electric current, firing new tingles and hunger and want down each and every nerve. "John… I don't want to know about it." *I so want to know about it.* She pressed her eyes shut. "You can't… We can't do anything about it. Nothing like this can happen again." *Even if we both want it.* She cleared her throat. "That's all I'm saying. Maybe it's best if we're not alone together."

He snorted. "I can control myself, Nat. If you want to stop, we stop."

Her cheeks were burning. "I do." He'd asked, twice, if she was sure. "I'm sorry."

He stepped forward, cradling her face and tilting her chin up. "Me, too. But not for the reasons you think." He shook his head. "If this is what you want, I'll respect your wishes."

This isn't what I want. She wanted him to tell her he loved her. More importantly, she wanted to be able to believe that he did, really, love her. Not the stability, the childcare, the beer, the companionship and lack of expectations he'd gotten accustomed to while staying with her.

"Don't give up on me." He pressed a kiss to her forehead. "Please." His hands slid away, and after grabbing his shirt, he slipped out the front door.

She heard John's mumble of "Yeah, yeah, good night to you, too" to Vlad and the crunch of his boots down the walkway. After the squeak of the opening and closing and the click of the gate latch catching, Nat gave in to the tears. She'd done the right thing—she knew it. John needed to figure out his own life, and she… Well, she needed to get hers in order, too. After all, having her heart broken wouldn't stop the IRS from taking away her business—and then how would she keep her home?

* * *

John took his time walking back to the Bear's House. He was reeling, confused and hurt. *What did I expect?* She'd ducked out of there, and he'd tracked her down.

He'd wanted to apologize for taking advantage of her, thank her for all she'd done for him and Leslie, then beg her to let him into her heart. Not that it'd worked out that way. Not that he was going to complain about winding up in her arms. *Hell, no.* Nothing had ever felt so right. Nothing. She'd invited him in and given herself over to him in a way he could never have imagined. Now he was supposed to forget about it?

That was never going to happen.

Part of him wanted her so bad, it hurt. The other part of him was scared senseless.

He didn't go back inside the Bear's House. The porch had a few high-top tables as well as some carved-out barrel chairs arranged in groups. He picked a chair and sat, stretching his leg out in front of him.

Nat had spoken some hard truths tonight, but he'd needed to hear them.

He didn't want to wind up like Benny Smith, spending his after-work hours propped up on a bar, reminiscing over stories that resembled nothing like the truth, while drinking away a third of his take-home. It was sad. Damn sad.

Enough was enough.

If he didn't stop feeling sorry for himself, he'd wind up exactly as his brother Hayden and that bastard Lt. Rogers had all said he would. A disappointment. A quitter. All talk and no action. This wasn't about proving them wrong. In the grand scheme of things, their opinions didn't matter. Years of jeers and insults hadn't made him want to do better.

But Nat had.

And...Leslie.

What did he want? That was a hell of a question. A few things immediately sprang to mind. Like being the man Nat believed he could be. A reliable, hard-working and decent man who owned his responsibilities. Easy? No. Fun? Hell, no. But it was time to grow up. *Nat's right about that, too.*

"Here you are," Kyle said, a beam of light spilling out into the dark as the front door of the Bear's House opened wide. "I thought you'd ditched us."

"He went after Natalie." Buzz followed, a little unsteady, and added, "Guess things didn't go well?"

John didn't answer. He'd been trying to zero in on what Nat had said, not on what he and Nat had done. If he thought about that, he'd forget about everything else... He could feel the soft swell of her breast in his hand and taste her on his lips. Want rolled over him, making his blood throb and his heart slam against his rib cage. The ache he had for Nat was like nothing he'd ever experienced before. He ran a hand over his face, pissed that he'd let things get so out of hand between them.

Kyle pulled one of the barrel chairs close and sat, sighing. "Lady trouble, huh? I'm no use to you, there."

John shot his brother a look. Not that anyone could see anything in the dark. He didn't want to have this conversation so he tried shutting it down. "This is Nat we're talking about."

Buzz snorted, almost falling into the barrel chair. "Damn straight. And she's hot. Or did you miss that?"

Hell, no. John swallowed. It was more than a little irritating to hear Buzz's take on Nat. "She's my best friend," he bit back. The same woman he'd had pinned against the front door, arching into him and stripping off his shirt with a single-minded purpose he'd been all too willing to help her with.

"That's good," Kyle said. "I think that's what makes a relationship stick. Friendship. If you don't have that, what do you have?"

It wasn't all that long ago that John would have laughed off the idea of a serious relationship with Nat. What they had was good—just the way it was. But now? There was nothing he wanted more. He did his best to block the image of her, eyes blazing as she twined her arms around his neck.

"I'll tell you what you have. Sex," Buzz offered. "A whole lot of it, too."

John had to chuckle.

Kyle did, too. "Sounds like a long and lasting relationship."

"You know me," Buzz teased. "Haven't found one worth keeping. Not that I'm looking."

John wasn't exactly looking, either, but that hadn't stopped these all too disconcerting and potent feelings from slamming him upside the head. Hard. So hard he was still seeing stars. Nat was his best friend but… She was so much more. Natalie Harris owned his heart. Period. That was fact. And while he was struggling with who he was, she was struggling with losing everything that mattered most to her.

He knew what was worrying her, and what had he done? Had he offered to help? Offered an ear? Acknowledged what she was going through? He hadn't done any of those things. He'd left her to deal with all of that—and heaped his self-perpetuated worries on top of that. *I'm a selfish bastard.*

"She's not interested?" Kyle asked. "In a relationship? I mean, more than friendship."

After the way he'd treated her? Self-loathing rolled over him. "I'm an unemployed, no-prospects, irresponsible single father with a bad attitude and authority problems." He paused. "Why the hell would she be?" He sighed. "Nat and I are just friends. That's all we will ever be." Because anything else would be...weird.

"Someone's feeling sorry for themselves..." Buzz chuckled.

"Stating facts." John sighed, enjoying this conversation less and less. "Facts that need changing." Here he was, claiming Nat was his best friend, all the while knowing he'd treated her poorly. He'd never been so ashamed of himself. Sitting here, really thinking about the month he'd spent with her... He was damned ashamed.

"Sounds like a heavy conversation for a bachelor party." This was from Hayden.

Where the hell had he come from?

"Hayden got here when you ran after Nat," Buzz whispered loudly, slurring his words.

"Thanks." John ran a hand over his face again, wincing as Hayden dragged another chair up to their grouping. This conversation was sure as hell *not* going to happen now.

"Oops, I didn't think that through. I guess you couldn't *run* after her." Buzz paused. "Not with your knee and all. But you get it."

"Yeah." John got it, but he wasn't going to let it get to him. Another fact: his limited mobility. He couldn't run. Not well.

"What about using your mechanic skills—you know, to solve the unemployment part of your description?" Kyle asked. "You spent the last eight years being an engineer equipment mechanic."

"How's that going to help out on the ranch?" he asked, shaking his head.

"Are you kidding?" Kyle laughed. "Hayden never buys anything new. He's too cheap."

"I'm not cheap," Hayden cut it, "I'm—"

"Yeah, yeah, you're *frugal*." Kyle used air quotes. "That's a nice way of saying *cheap*. What I'm saying is there's always something that needs fixing."

John shook his head. "What about Sven?" Sven Drummond had been the Granite Falls mechanic for years. That man had known how to talk to an engine. It had been Sven and Bear, good friends, who had taken John under their wing—to keep him out of trouble and teach him all about the internal workings of an engine, a transmission and anything else useful—beyond changing out spark plugs and doing oil changes.

"Sven moved to Las Vegas—what?—two years ago?" Hayden asked. "We have to drive to Fredericksburg or Johnson City. Not a cheap tow."

John sat back, mulling this information.

"Wouldn't take much to get the old south barn usable," Kyle suggested. "Of course, Bear's got a shop sitting empty on his property, too."

John didn't pretend not to understand what his brother was implying. "I don't want to drag Nat into this." From here on out, Nat was no longer going to be his safety net. No exceptions. "I've done that enough already."

There was a momentary silence. He'd dragged her into the mess of his life and expected her to take care of him… Maybe she was right—maybe he had been using her. *There is no* maybe *about it*. Intentional or not, he had used her.

"She's a good friend. She's always been a good friend to you," Kyle said.

John nodded. *I don't want to lose her.* "It's getting late," he said, standing. "I should get home. Mom's got her hands full." Leslie always got extra fussy after dark. According to the book, she had colic. Meaning she'd cry and fuss and wriggle until she wore herself out. He still felt awkward holding her, and he knew his humming couldn't compare to Nat's, but he was trying. It was all he could do. Now it was up to him to try to fix things— with himself and with Nat. All he could do was hope that the damage he'd done to their friendship could be repaired. If it couldn't? Well, what the hell would he do without Nat in his life?

Chapter Twelve

"How much?" Nat asked, balancing the phone between her shoulder and cheek as she scribbled down the numbers for each motorcycle. "What about the 1929 Indian Scout?" Which had been Bear's favorite. He'd taken such good care of it, keeping it polished and the engine purring in case he decided to take it out. Not that he ever did.

"If we get the right collector, we're looking at upward of forty thousand dollars," Harry said, the sound of pages flipping. "One went for fifty-three thousand, but that was in top condition. What's Bear's look like?"

"I'd say excellent, but I'm not one to judge, Harry." And she didn't want to get her hopes up. She was still having a hard time selling Grampa Bear's bikes. Each one of them had a story and a meaning; each one was a treasure to him. And now she was selling them off to the highest bidder...
But what choice do I have?

"Take some pictures for me. Every angle, in good lighting. And I mean all the details, dings, scratches, you name it. Do you have any paper-work on them?" Harry's voice was muffled now and then, like he was moving around while he was talking.

"I'm sure Bear has it all in his office." Another thing she'd learned about Bear: keep anything that might be of later significance. From paperwork to her school projects to the bill of sale and receipt for every vehicle he'd ever owned through his life, motorcycles included. "I'll see what I can find."

"Good." Harry sighed. "Mecum Auctions is having a big sale in two weeks. If we can get the paperwork found and some good pictures together, really quick, I can try to get us added to the list-ings. The auction site is already up and running, so the sooner, the better."

"Two weeks?" Nat stared out the kitchen win-dow, her heart in her throat. "I'll get started." It was Sunday, meaning the Bear's House was closed, and she could focus all of her energy on getting this done.

"All righty, then. I'll be waiting." Harry paused. "Have a good day, Nat. We'll get this sorted out."

"Thank you so much for your help, Harry." What would she do without the man?

"Oh, now, Nat, you know what Bear did for me." Harry cleared his throat. "I wouldn't be alive today if he hadn't knocked some sense into me."

She swallowed hard. Bear hadn't always been on the right side of the law. He'd drunk too much and never backed away from a fight. But then he'd had a bad accident, one that almost left him with serious injuries—enough to shake him straight. For the next two years, he'd done his best to bring his riding buddies around. He reformed a few and he lost a few, but he said it was worth it if it helped getting one of them healthy. Harry was one of the reformed ones. "Bear loved you," she said.

"Well…well…" Harry cleared his throat. "You send me that info, Nat. I'll talk to you soon."

They both hung up, and she stared for a moment at the old phone. Bear had refused to give up their landline—or his 1970s avocado-green telephone with its twelve-foot-long coiled cord. As a result, she'd never purchased a cell. Now she wouldn't have to worry about keeping herself occupied, taking pictures and sending copies on any original paperwork her grandfather kept. Upside, it would prevent her from missing Leslie and thinking about the near catastrophe that had taken place in the front hallway two nights before. Because every time she stopped, it was there—John. John's kiss. John's touch. John's scent. John…shirtless and breathless and pressed up against her until she'd been on the verge of giving in.

Right there.

In the middle of the hallway.

Against the front door…of her grandfather's home.

A home I'll lose if I don't get this information to Harry.

Grampa Bear would give her a talking-to about how moony-eyed and distracted she was getting over a boy. *Man.* A big, muscular, scarred, manly man. *A man that needs to get himself together.* Something she'd made crystal clear to him…while she was putting her shirt back on. She shook her head. Her grandfather adored John Mitchell. But she had a hard time believing her grandfather would be pleased with the way either one of them was behaving. He'd been a practical man; he wouldn't tolerate this sort of drama.

Right. No drama. She was pretty sure the IRS wouldn't tolerate it, either. She ran a hand over her hair, fluffing the uneven layers and smoothing the long-angled bangs along her jaw. *Like I need to get myself together.* She had a plan; now she needed to put it into action.

It didn't take long to locate Bear's camera—safely stowed in the hard carrying case at the bottom of his closet. It was digital and high-powered, one of the last Christmas presents she'd given him. As far as she knew, he'd never actually used it because he'd been worried about how expensive it was. *Hopefully all the high-tech bells and whistles will make the motorcycles look their very best.*

She headed out the back door, the camera bag in hand. "Hi, Vlad." She waved at the oversize raccoon. Vlad chittered and skittered down the tree to trail after her across the overgrown backyard to Bear's shop. "Coming inside?" she asked, propping open the door with a large rock.

Vlad said something in raccoon but didn't follow her in.

She switched on the lights, rolled up the metal doors and flipped on the massive overhead shop fan. Vlad peered inside through one of the roll-up doors, ears cocked and nose twitching. "What do you think?" She turned, taking in the meticulous organization her grandfather had taken such pride in.

Vlad rose up on his toes, his nose wiggling with more energy.

"A lot to take in, right?" She sighed. "Let's get to work." She put the camera on the desk in the back corner of the shop and began searching through the filing cabinets for any documentation that Harry might find useful. After an hour of looking, she'd found all the paperwork she needed, taken pictures of each and stored them away again for safekeeping. She scrolled through the photos. "Looks good to me." She glanced at Vlad, who'd ventured just inside the shop and was sniffing at the covered motorcycles. "Yep, those are next." She smiled at Vlad, who sat back and looked at her, cocking his head to one side. "Should we start with that one?"

Vlad yawned.

"Sorry. This will take a while, so make yourself at home." She leaned against the desk and drank most of the bottle of water she'd brought with her. "This place is full of good memories."

"You can say that again." John stood in the doorway. John? *Here?* Now? In a cowboy hat, no less… He'd always looked good in a cowboy hat. Her heart had already picked up, but then she noticed Leslie strapped to his chest in some sort of carrier, and her pulse all but took flight.

Alpha stood at John's side, but as soon as he saw her, the dog trotted over to her.

"Hey, Alpha." She crouched, giving the animal a good rub behind the ears. "How are you, big man?"

"Happy to see you, from the looks of it." There was a smile in John's voice.

I love his smile. Not that she was going to look to verify he was smiling. That wouldn't be smart. She sighed, disappointed in how quickly he got to her. All of her hard work *not* thinking about him went out the window… *Why are you here?* Today, of all days, she didn't need distracting, so of course, he'd show up now that she had things to do and not much time to do them in. "Where did you come from?" she asked.

Leslie wiggled, catching Nat's full attention. Was it her imagination or had she grown? It'd been a week… Just a week. But Nat had been painfully aware of Leslie's absence. She loved that baby girl, and right now, she ached to cradle her close.

"A few miles on the other side of town, down Country Road 380, then a half a mile down a long gravel drive—"

She tore her gaze from the baby—looking, instead, at John. "I know where Mitchell ranch is. I mean, why are you here?"

"Oh." His smile faded a bit. "I tried calling." He patted Leslie's back slowly.

"I've been out here." She crossed her arms over her chest, hating how empty they felt. "I… I've got some things to do."

He stepped inside and looked around. "Can I help?"

"No. I've got it." She shook her head, her gaze meeting his. And just like that, those light brown eyes started weaving a spell… Drawing her in, clouding her reason and wrapping warmth around her heart. When it came to John, it was impossible to keep him out of her heart. "Thank you, though."

And Leslie. If he was trying to test her, it was working. Leslie was here, in all her adorable, tiny cuteness, and he was holding her… *What does this mean?* Why did it matter? It didn't. She stiffened her spine. "I've got it," she repeated.

John stared down at the top of Leslie's head, looking almost dejected.

Instead of sending him on his way, she found herself asking, "Was there… What brought you all the way out here?" It wasn't like her home was close to…anything. There had to be a reason he was here. For some ridiculous reason, she felt a flicker of hope in the pit of her stomach.

"I think I left—" he broke off, glancing her way "—Alpha's food."

Nat frowned. "You did?" She knew Alpha's food was gone, along with every bit of evidence that John and Leslie had ever stayed with her. Coming home from the bar to a perfectly clean home had been a slap in the face. She never thought she'd miss empty beer bottles or canisters of formula lining her kitchen counter or giant dog-food bags in the corner, but she had. She did. And since she knew for a fact that the fifty-pound bag of dog food was not still sitting in the corner of her kitchen, there had to be another reason for John's visit. "Alpha's food?"

Alpha sat at her side, ears perked up, staring at John.

John opened his mouth, then closed it.

"Why are you really here, John?" she asked, hands on her hips, willing her rising hope aside.

There was nothing to hope for. Until John had found his path, there was nothing to hope for.

Leslie wiggled and grunted, a squeak emerging—then building.

"Dammit." He stared down at Leslie, patting a little more firmly.

Leslie's cry tugged at Nat's heart. Hard. "Need a hand?" she asked.

"No." He shook his head, bracing Leslie close, and fumbling with the clasps on the side of the carrier.

"I don't mind, John. I've missed her." There was no harm in admitting that. She did. She ached for the feel of Leslie in her arms. The louder Leslie's cries became, the sharper that ache became. "Please?"

John wasn't sure what to do. Could he use a hand with Leslie? Yes. But he'd wanted to show her he was figuring things out with his daughter—that he wasn't as needy as he had been. He was still needy, of course, but not…dependent.

But now… Well, it hurt to hear her say she'd missed Leslie. He hurt because she hurt. "I bet she's missed you, too." He'd meant to tease, but looking into her eyes, it took effort to get the words out.

Nat's gaze dropped from his as she helped unbuckle the carrier. The instant Leslie was in her arms, Nat's smile was pure joy. Free and light and all-consuming. Like holding the baby was the greatest gift she'd ever been given. "Hi, little one. How are you? I think you've gotten bigger. Have you?"

There was a reverence to her voice that washed over him. She loved his baby girl—that was obvious. She'd loved Leslie before he had. But now... well, he no longer denied Leslie was his daughter or that she'd found a way into his heart. Like Nat. Nat and Leslie. They mattered most. It struck him, right then, that this was right. This was the way it should be. The three of them. Like this.

It was such a jarring thought he shook his head. What was he doing? What was he thinking?

"John? Did you hear me?" Nat was studying him, Leslie cradled in her arms.

"What?" he asked. "Sorry."

"You were going to tell me why you're here?" She smiled down at Leslie. Leslie, who stared up at Nat with wide eyes.

Right. Back to the hard stuff. He'd come here with a purpose, one he wasn't going to get derailed from. "I wanted to apologize." He cleared his throat. "Again."

She didn't look at him. "It's nothing. Nothing happened."

Happened? He paused. "What do you think I'm apologizing for?" Did he really want to know?

Her blue eyes met his then. "Friday night? Here..."

Inside?" Her cheeks were a deep red. "The...the kiss?"

Kiss, huh? It'd been a hell of a lot more than that. *I remember. Every detail.* And he wasn't about to apologize for that. She'd wanted it. He'd wanted it. If she hadn't stopped things, he knew exactly where things would have ended. In Nat's bed. He'd thought about that a lot, a whole hell of a lot. That was part of the problem. Once he started thinking about what had almost happened between them, it was damn near impossible to stop. *Not the sort of thing I need to be thinking about right now.* He ran a hand over his face. "No." When his eyes met hers, there was no ignoring the pull between them. It was there, alive and humming.

Her eyes widened, the red in her cheeks deepening. "No?" It was a hoarse whisper. She blinked several times, then went back to looking at Leslie, running one finger along the baby's cheek. "Then...what?"

He swallowed. It was now or never. "When I was staying at your place, Alpha might have knocked some stuff onto the floor..." He shook his head. *Don't lie.* From the way she was looking at him, she wasn't buying it, anyway. He sighed. "Okay, I might have gone through your mail."

Nat blinked—several times. "You...you what?"

"I didn't mean to. I just..." He sighed. *Better to get to the point.* "I know about the back taxes and the IRS and the possible property forfeiture, and I want to help."

Nat was staring at him, all the color draining from her face.

"I am sorry, Nat. I am." He swallowed. "But I can't stand by and do nothing… You've helped me, so much. I want to help."

Nat kept staring, those blue eyes wide and assessing.

"You're mad?" He swallowed.

She didn't answer.

"Nat." He stepped forward, reaching for her. "I *am* sorry. Can you forgive me? Not just for snooping—I know that was a jerk move, I do—but for the situation you're in. It's not fair."

Nat blinked, her lips pressed tight.

"What can I do?" He couldn't take it. He figured she'd be upset, but this? He didn't know how to handle this. Her silence was all too easy to read into. Not so good things, at that. "Say something, Nat. You're killing me here."

She shook her head.

He frowned, his chest tightening. "You won't forgive me?" He couldn't breathe then. She had every right to reject his apology—but it didn't make it any easier for him.

"No." She patted Leslie, turning all of her attention to the baby. "I… Why didn't you say something?"

"You didn't, so I didn't want to intrude." He paused, his breath escaping on a hiss. "Let's cut the bull, okay? I've been a selfish prick, Nat. I know it, and you know it. I should have said something. And, dammit, I'm sorry for that, too."

Nat was blinking a lot now, her gaze fixed on Leslie. But he saw them. Tears. Silent, but undeniably there. She wasn't sobbing. Hell, she wasn't making a sound. The only evidence that she was crying were the tears streaming down her face.

"Nat…" He reached for her. "Whoa, now. Hey, now. I didn't mean to make you cry."

She shook her head. "I'm not," she sniffed.

"Um…" He paused. "Nat."

"I'm *not* crying," she argued.

"What are those things on your face?" he asked. "And how do I make it stop?"

"It's stopping now." She laughed a little. "Not that I was crying. Not really, anyway."

"Fine. I'll play along." But then he stopped himself. *No, dammit.* He'd been playing along since he got home. He'd known something was going on with her almost the whole damn time, and he'd kept his mouth shut because he thought that's what she wanted and…he didn't want to deal with it. That wasn't how this worked. A relationship was give-and-take, sharing each other's burdens, lifting each other up and holding on to one another when they were down. But turning his back, willfully ignoring her troubles? *That behavior was stopping, right here and now.* It didn't matter that he was way outside his comfort zone. Nat needed help, and he was going to step up. "The thing is I don't think I can play along, Nat. This isn't a little problem. This is one of those life-altering situations you shouldn't have to handle alone." He swallowed. "I'm here. For whatever you need—or whatever that means... I'm here."

Nat shook her head. "I appreciate that, John, but you have your own—"

"Problems? You're right, I do." He sighed. "And you know all about them. You've helped me through a lot of them. And Friday night, you gave me the slap in the face that I needed. I'm here to return the favor."

"When you put it like that, how can I refuse?" But her attempt to joke was overshadowed by the catch to her breath when she said *refuse.*

"You can't." He held her shoulders now, smiling down at Leslie. "I won't let you. Let me help."

Nat drew in a deep breath, staring up at him. There were tears on those long lashes of hers. Tears on her cheeks making her eyes shine...

"No more tears," he whispered, aching for her. Not just to pull her close and kiss her—mindful of Leslie between them, of course—but to give her what she needed. "Tell me what needs doing."

"John." She sighed, staring at his chest. "What

I said Friday… I meant it. I don't want my situation overshadowing what…you need to do for you."

"I know." He nodded. "And I'm working on that. But you can't expect me to spend every hour of every day working on myself and my goals and my wants and future, when I know you're at risk of losing…everything that matters to you." He smiled. "Being here, helping out, is working on myself. I'm putting someone else first for a bit. Someone who I care about." *Someone I love.*

He wasn't here because the two of them were meant to be together, even if they were. He was here because Nat needed help, and he was going to help her. And if there was anything he could do to stop more tears or prevent more loss, he'd do it. "Nat." He shook her, gently, until she looked him in the eye. "Don't shut me out."

Her blue eyes searched long and hard before she said "Okay" so softly he wasn't sure he'd heard correctly.

"Okay?" he repeated. "Good. Where do we start?" He let her go then, rubbing his hands together.

"Pictures." She nodded at the row of covered motorcycles. "I've been talking to Harry James."

"Bear's friend?" John vaguely remembered the man. There were quite a few who'd been touched by Bear's gruff yet encouraging support. John was one of them. He had nothing but fond memories of the tattoo-covered, leather-wearing, long-haired, bearded man with earrings that all of Granite Falls knew of—but not all of Granite Falls approved of.

Those who didn't approve of Bear? They didn't know the man. Likely, they'd taken one look at his hardened exterior and decided he was up to no good. Maybe that was true, but John had only known the soft-spoken, generous and forgiving Bear. Bear always had a seat at his table and real-world advice to those lost or losing their way. John had been one of them.

"He thinks there's a chance I could make almost the whole two hundred and eleven thousand dollars off the sale of the bikes."

"That's good, isn't it?" he asked, noting her less than enthusiastic tone.

"It is." She nodded. "It's good. It's just… I don't have a lot left of him, you know? Selling these? It feels wrong. Cold, even." She glanced at him. "I miss him so much, John. Since he died, I've been alone."

That hurt. Bear had been gone for three years. John had been deployed for the first one, in medical facilities and rehabilitation for a good deal of the second, but he could have been there—should have been there—for the last few months or so.

Not that I'd have been much use. He'd been all self-pity, drinking and one-night stands with sympathetic women back then. Leslie was the living proof of that. He couldn't go back and change things, but he could make sure things were different—better— moving forward.

"You're not alone now," he vowed, emotion grabbing him by the throat. *I'm not going anywhere.*

There was the hint of a smile on Nat's lips. "If you're sure—"

"I'm sure." He nodded. "I've never been so sure of anything in my whole life, Nat. Tell me what you need. I'll move heaven and earth to make it happen."

Her smile grew. "How about we start with some pictures? We can save the whole moving heaven and earth as a last resort."

"Deal." John nodded. "Camera?"

"On the desk." She nodded, bouncing Leslie in her arms. "Be careful, though. Vlad was poking around over there, and knowing him, he might jump out and surprise you."

"That reminds me." He picked up the camera, then faced her. "I have something for you. Or Vlad."

Her brows rose. "You do?"

"Another hammock swing." He watched her expression shift, from surprise to real happiness. "Knowing you, Vlad will continue to hog your swing, and you'll continue to let him. Now, you'll each have your own." Nat's smile was megawatt. Just enough to make his heart near trip over itself.

"You hear that, Leslie? Your daddy got me a present. For me and Vlad." She cooed to the baby. "A very thoughtful present. Your daddy's a softy, you know that? He tries to act all big and strong and tough, but deep down, he's a big ol' softy." She started humming what sounded a lot like Billy Idol's "White Wedding."

I'm a softy, all right—for you. If Harry James thought selling Bear's bikes would get Nat out of this mess, then that's what they'd do. He understood Nat's reticence about selling them, of course: they'd been a big part of who Bear was. But her grandfather would be the first person to understand. He'd wanted Nat to have a secure and happy life, and that's what auctioning off his bikes would do. He pulled the tarp off the first motorcycle and started taking pictures. The sooner this was done, the better. Nat had been dealing with this for who knew how long. She deserved a break. She deserved happiness. Nothing was going to stop him from helping her get it.

Chapter Thirteen

Nat had envisioned this day going very differently. She'd expected some tears: she was inventorying her grandfather's life to sell. Not exactly the best way to reconnect with the most important man in her life. One of them, anyway. But somehow, John had shown up with Leslie and Alpha and smiled and laughed and shared stories until she'd had no choice but to cheer up.

Now, Alpha and Vlad were sitting four feet apart from each other in the middle of the open garage door, Leslie was sound asleep in the infant carrier John had collected from his truck and she and John were finishing up with the pictures.

"I admit, this one is my favorite." She ran her hand along the leather seat of the 1943 BMW R75 military motorcycle and sidecar combo he'd acquired after she came to live with him. "I took my first motorcycle ride in this. I was ten." She smiled at John.

"All braids and overalls." John nodded. "I remember. That helmet just about covered your face up."

"I remember, too—you pulling on my braids and teasing me for my overalls." She shot him a look.

"You were unknown. I had to figure you out." He shrugged. "You punching me in the face set me straight, didn't it?"

She nodded, laughing at the memory. "The look on your face."

"Yeah, well, it wasn't every day I got my bell rung by someone half my size." John chuckled. "You were a fighter back then."

I still am—when I need to be. There were a few skills she'd held on to from her mother and her string of revolving boyfriends. Such as how to protect herself. One of the boyfriends, Guy, had owned a boxing studio. She'd gone a few times, when her mother was working late or shopping or didn't want to deal with Nat. The boxers had filtered their language or acted differently when she was around—she'd been part of the decor. Slumped in one corner, her chin on her knees, she would watch huge, muscular people duck and weave, jump rope and, occasionally, beat the crap out of each other. "I still know how to pack a punch—if I need to."

"I'll keep that in mind." John rubbed his chin, his light brown eyes narrowing. "Maybe we should have a charity boxing match."

"You're hilarious. However, that might not be

necessary." She patted the seat of the WWII motorcycle. "Harry said this could bring in a lot of money." Her smile faded. "But it's the one I'm having the hardest time giving up." She shrugged, horrified to realize she was close to tears, again. "Before I got here, he'd take long rides on the weekend, raise some hell and enjoy being a handsome, single man. When I got older, I heard all the stories. Well, probably not all of them. But a lot of them. Listening to him and his buddies, I couldn't help but wonder if he missed that, you know? Being the wild Bear I'd heard so many stories about." She smiled at John. "When I got here, I never saw that side of him. The wild side. He was just my grandfather. A little unusual, maybe, but my grampa Bear." She paused, staring down at the bike. "I'll never forget the look on his face when we took this out that first time. That was when I knew he was happiest then, on the road."

John crossed to her, resting his hand on the seat beside hers. "He was happiest when he was with you."

Nat looked up at him. "You think so?"

"I know so." He was studying her. "Maybe hold this one back? Only sell it if you have to?"

"It could bring in over a hundred thousand dollars, John." She sighed. "I can't afford to pass up that sort of money."

"Right." John shook his head, the ringing of his cell phone making her jump.

It was different now, knowing Emily wasn't coming back. Her heart wasn't immediately launched into orbit and her stomach wasn't churning with nausea-inducing fear. But she remembered what he'd said about cell phones. "An emergency? Everything okay?"

"I gave in. Damn things might be a nuisance, but they sure come in handy." John chuckled, pulling his phone from his pocket. "It's Mom." He held up the phone. "Hey, Mom."

Nat picked up the tarp, shook it out and carefully draped it over the WWII motorcycle. All she had to do now was download the images onto her computer and email them to Harry. If luck was on her side, he'd get the bikes into the auction and she'd make the money she needed to save her home and the Bear's House.

"I'll ask." He held the phone away. "Join us for dinner?"

Nat shook her head. "I need to get this to Harry."

"I'll wait. She's making pot roast." John waited. "Your favorite."

"Not for me?" Why on earth would Jan go through all that trouble?

He nodded.

"How can I say no?" She looked down at her grease streaked jeans and shirt.

"We'll be there," he said into the phone. "An hour? Sounds good." He hung up. "That should give you plenty of time to get the pictures to Harry."

"And take a shower?" She rolled the first of the three large garage doors shut as quietly as possible. She moved to the third door, smiling as Vlad and Alpha sat watching her, but neither of them moving. "Okay, boys, I have to close this one, too."

Alpha stood up and trotted into the yard, nosing around in the tall grass.

Vlad watched Alpha, but then he turned his back to her, showed his teeth and clicked. He moved in a circle, scratched his ear, then ran across the grass and into his tree.

"I guess that was his way of telling you he wasn't going because you told him to, he was going because he decided to?" John was laughing.

"I see you're fluent in Vlad." She rolled the final door shut. "But as far as roommates go, he's pretty low-key."

"Not leaving beer bottles all over? Or leaving babies on your front porch?" John teased.

Nat shook her head. "Not so far." She smiled at Leslie. It was on the tip of her tongue to ask him about Leslie. Had he made any decisions? Yes, she was his daughter, but that didn't mean John wasn't still considering adoption. *Not that it's any of my business.* "She's so beautiful, John." Her gaze swiveled his way.

Up until now, it had been a good day—a happy day. John was more like his old self. The John she was madly, unconditionally and passionately in love with.

"Beautiful. But still a banshee." He winked, his warm, tawny gaze pinned on her.

"I still don't approve of that nickname." She sighed. "So things are good?" She turned off one of the overhead lights, waiting for him.

He picked up Leslie's car seat by the handle, but the baby didn't stir. "I think so. I've been thinking about things. Making plans. Adulting. All of it." He headed to the door of the shop. "What are you going to do with the shop? It's a hell of a facility, Nat." With a final look around, he stepped outside to wait for her. "You ever think about renting it out? To a mechanic?"

She flipped off the last light, pulled the door closed and joined him outside. "No, I never have." Before he'd opened the Bear's House, her grandfather had been a mechanic. Growing up, there'd always been a car or motorcycle here—something he and his buddies would work on, tinkering with it until they were all satisfied.

"You should." He glanced her way. "Or you could sell all of his tools. He has a pretty big collection in there—the sort of stuff every good mechanic needs. And then some. I'm no expert, but I'd guess there's several thousand dollars in tools in there. Either way, it might be another way to make money."

"I guess so." She nodded. It was good to have more options. "Know anyone on the market?"

"Maybe."

Was it her imagination, or did he sound excited?

As nice as it was for him to come up with other fundraising ideas for her, her thoughts circled back around to Leslie. It appeared that he was more comfortable with his daughter now. He'd given her a bottle and changed her diaper over the course of the afternoon—without asking for any help from Nat. It had filled Nat's heart with hope. Of course, she'd stepped in, anyway. Holding Leslie, feeding and changing her, had filled the ache in her heart she'd been struggling with since John and Leslie had left.

The cold, hard truth of the matter was John's decision had nothing to do with her. She wanted Leslie to stay, but what if John was right? What if he wasn't able to be the sort of father Leslie deserved? *But...he is.* Nat knew it, deep down. John would be the best father. Adoring and patient and kind and loving. Or was she seeing what she wanted to see?

"I can get these pics downloaded, if you want to take a shower," John offered, holding open the back door of the house.

"You don't mind?" She set the camera on the table.

"Nope. Use the computer in Bear's office?" he asked, holding the car seat like it weighed next to nothing.

Leslie chose that moment to yawn, instantly entrancing Nat. Her little face squished up, those rosebud lips went round, and her whole body stretched and wiggled. "She's so precious. I could just watch her all day." She smiled, watching the baby's head recline against the padded headrest, drifting back into sleep. "I'd get nothing done."

"You can say that again." John nodded.

"About her being precious?" Nat watched him. "Or about getting nothing done?"

"Both." He shrugged. "She's still a little banshee baby when she wants to be."

His smile was so warm and bright it stole the air from Nat's lungs. It wasn't fair. None of this was fair. Why couldn't Leslie be her baby? Why couldn't John love her? Why couldn't they raise Leslie together—as a real family?

"Nat?" He was frowning now. "What's wrong?"

She shook her head. "I… I can't help but wish that things were different, that's all." With a final glance at Leslie she said, "I'll take a quick shower," and headed down the hall to her room. With any luck, she'd figure out a way to excuse herself from this dinner disaster. While she appreciated Jan Mitchell's kindness, she wasn't sure she could keep smiling through dinner without learning if Leslie's life had been decided. If John had decided to give Leslie up, would Nat be able to respect his decision or would she be brokenhearted all over again?

John knew something had changed the minute they'd stepped inside the house. He couldn't pinpoint what exactly he'd said or done, but Nat was shutting down. His suspicions were confirmed when she half-heartedly tried to back out of going to dinner. But once she'd sent the email to Harry with the link to the documents and photos, there'd been no reason for her not to come.

The ride to the ranch had been long. Leslie's wailing had made it that much longer.

"There she is. In full Banshee-Baby mode." He winked at Nat, relieved when the roof of his sprawling childhood home came into sight. "A few more seconds, Leslie. Try not to explode."

"You haven't come up with a better nickname?" Nat asked.

"I think Banshee Baby fits." He parked the truck.

Nat's sigh was pure disapproval. "You get her, I'll follow." Nat opened the passenger door and climbed down, holding it wide so Alpha could jump down, too.

John unclipped Leslie's car seat and hefted it from the truck. His sudden step backward twisted his knee and had him wincing with pain, but he drew in several deep breaths until he could manage. He pushed the door shut and walked, a little slower than usual, to where Nat waited on the front porch.

She tucked her hair behind one ear and rolled up on her toes, impatient. But John got a little sidetracked by the picture she made. She wore jeans that hugged her hips and a pale blue shirt with small white stitched flowers all over it that was both sweet and sexy. Just like Nat. Buzz had said she was hot. *Damned if he hadn't called that one.*

"You look beautiful, Nat."

Nat's eyes widened.

"You do." He stared down at her, that ache returning. An ache only Nat could cause. What would she do if he pulled her into his arms? Right here, right now?

"Thank you." She swallowed.

"You're welcome." He continued to stare, until Leslie's fusses began creeping back up into the range that sent Alpha sprinting—he rarely sprinted—to the end of the porch. "I think she's hungry."

Nat was all smiles for Leslie.

He opened the front door to the chaos that was his family home. Weston, Hayden's little boy, was chasing after Kyle's twin girls with a large rubber snake. Greer, the baby of the bunch, was on a play mat with her mother, Skylar, right in the middle of the room. The baby girl was up on her knees, rocking back and forth, watching the three older kids with a wide, toothless grin.

"Hi, John," Skylar greeted him. "Someone's ready for dinner."

John nodded.

"Poor thing." Lizzie greeted them, "Hi, John. Hi, Natalie." She paused. "We're in the middle of potty training so you'll have to excuse me." And she went hurrying after Weston.

"Never a dull moment." Kyle waved them in. "You good?" he asked, wincing when Leslie hit an especially high note.

"We will be just fine." From the corner of his eye, John saw his brothers' dogs run for cover, just like Alpha had done. Not only was his family home full of children, it was chock-full of canines. Alpha tolerated the other dogs, but being the old man of the group, he tended to stick close to John or find someplace quiet and away from the other dogs. "Not so sure about the dogs, though." He set the car seat on the coffee table, unclipped Leslie and lifted her. "You're okay, little girl." Carefully, like he'd seen Nat and his mother and the handful of people in parenting videos he'd watched on YouTube do, he cradled his daughter against his chest. "I know you're hungry."

"I'll get it," Skylar offered. "Kyle? Can you watch Greer?"

"Can do." Kyle nodded. "She's not crawling yet so she's not really going anywhere," he added in an aside to Nat. "How's it going, Nat?"

"Pretty good." Nat looked a little shell-shocked.

He knew the feeling. He remembered the house being a hub of activity growing up, but not like this. Since he'd moved home, the place seemed to be in constant motion. Until the sun went down, more likely than not, there were little ones underfoot and constant chatter in a wide range of volumes. Leslie's cry pitched high. "You win," he whispered, smiling at her. "Hold on. Aunt Skylar's coming."

While he had yet to feel 100 percent comfortable with the women his brothers had married, he liked them well enough. Lizzie, Hayden's wife, never met a stranger. When she talked, she came alive—all hand gestures and expressive features. How Hayden had wound up with her he didn't know. As best as John could tell, Lizzie and Hayden were perfect opposites. Thankfully, Hayden's son, Weston, favored Lizzie in mannerisms and disposition.

Skylar was more reserved. She was a good mother to her girls, loving and patient in a way that inspired John. He could barely manage one tiny baby—this woman had been raising three on her own for years. Skylar and Kyle were two peas in a pod. Easy-going. Warm. Sincere.

"Welcome, Natalie," his mother gushed, emerging from behind the kitchen counter to wrap Nat up in a hug. "I'm so glad you could make it."

"Thank you for having me. And making pot roast. I didn't realize it would be a family dinner. Are you sure I'm not intruding?" The discomfort was clear on her face.

"Of course not." His mother smiled. "You are family, Nat. Don't forget that. It's been too long."

"Can I do anything to help?" Nat offered.

"Here you go." Skylar appeared, baby bottle in hand.

"Thanks." John offered the bottle to Nat. "You can feed her?" he asked. "I can clean up?"

Nat nodded, all of the unease and awkwardness melting from her face once Leslie was cradled close. "It's all right, little one," she cooed.

He hadn't expected that the sight of Nat, holding Leslie, could make his heart so full. It was there, as real and unwavering as ever. That certainty. This was everything he wanted. Right here. *Nope. Hold on.* This was easy. This was comfortable. Nat made things better. She always had. That's all this was, nothing more. He needed to keep reminding himself of that. But at the moment, he couldn't get over the way his mother and sister-in-law were watching him. More like staring. He didn't like it. Not one bit. "I'll go shower." He shook his head, his gaze bouncing from Nat to Leslie as he wiggled Leslie's foot before heading down the hall to his old bedroom.

The whole time he was showering, he could hear Nat's voice clearly, ringing in his head. *You need to figure things out. Get your stuff straight. Know what you want. You have to grow up, John. Like it or not, you have responsibilities—the kind that won't go away.*

He was figuring things out. He'd given the south barn a once-over, and as far as he could tell, it made the most sense for him. Bear's shop was nice, but he didn't want to complicate things with Nat. That didn't mean he wouldn't buy every single one of Bear's tools and equipment. He would—and pay top dollar for them, too. Nat would be helping him out, and he'd be helping her out, without invading her personal space. He didn't want to do that. Not this time. This time, things had to be different. If they were going to have any sort of future, it had to be one where they were on equal footing.

With that in mind, he'd decided to talk to Hayden about using the south barn for a shop. The only concern he had with the whole setup was the talk he'd have to have with Hayden. After that? No worries.

He dressed, shaved and headed back into the open-concept great room and kitchen where everyone was gathered. Between Kyle and Skylar's twins, Mya and Brynn, and Hayden and Lizzie's

Weston making circles around the great room and his mother attempting to have a conversation over the children's giggles and squeals, John couldn't help but wonder if this was a glimpse into his future.

Kids. Noise. Laughter. Constant commotion... He could think of worse things.

Nat was seated at the end of the kitchen table chatting with his mother. Little Leslie rested in the crook of Nat's arm, working on her bottle.

"Makes a nice picture," Kyle said, elbowing him.

If he didn't put a stop to this now, he'd never hear the end of it. "She is a fr—"

"Nope." Kyle shook his head. "Not buying it. Not one bit. Not with you looking at her like that. Sorry, little brother, but the truth is written all over your face."

"You need to get your eyes checked." John brushed past Kyle, heading straight for the kitchen. His pace slowed once he spied Hayden, leaning against the kitchen counter, apparently taking part in the conversation.

"Feel better?" his mother asked. "You certainly look better. And you shaved. Finally."

He ran a hand along his jaw. "Don't care for the scruffy look?"

"I'll take you however I get you." His mother was all smiles. "Nat was just filling us in on everything."

Everything? As in his stay with her? Her IRS

troubles? Leslie's arrival? What, exactly, did *everything* mean? He cleared his throat. "Should I be worried?" he teased, casting a quick glance Nat's way.

Nat smiled. "No."

"Wait, now. Is there something to be worried about?" Kyle asked, propping himself up on his elbows to wait.

Nat kept right on smiling. "No."

John didn't have an answer for that. Not an honest one, anyway. Considering the way he was feeling about Nat—even though he was still trying to pretend he wasn't feeling a thing—he *was* beginning to get worried.

"She was telling us about needing to sell the motorcycles. And that crook of an accountant." His mother's smile was all sympathy. "Such an awful thing, Natalie. I had no idea."

"No. Nat's really good at keeping things to herself." John nodded. "She doesn't like to burden people."

Nat stiffened, her smile tightening.

"That was meant as a compliment." John pulled out the chair next to her and sat, trying to catch her eye. "I've never known anyone as selfless as Natalie Harris."

Nat shot a look his way.

He held up both hands. "No sarcasm. I mean it."

"What the hell is happening?" Kyle asked.

"John, without sarcasm? This is going to take some getting used to."

"Look who's talking," Hayden sounded off finally. "Is there anything we can do to help, Natalie?"

John glanced his big brother's way. Hayden might not think much of him, but he wasn't as quick to pigeonhole the rest of the human population. *Just me.*

Nat shook her head. "Keep your fingers and toes crossed that the bikes sell for what Harry's estimated. If they do, everything will be fine."

"If not?" Hayden asked.

Nat went back to studying Leslie. "I'll look at what else I can sell off."

Now was as good a time as ever. "I'd like to buy Bear's tools."

"You would?" Nat and his mother said in unison.

He chuckled. "I would. My older brothers informed me that Sven moved on and that Granite Falls is short a mechanic." He pointed at himself. "I happen to be a mechanic."

"A good mechanic." Kyle nodded.

"Bear thought so," Nat agreed.

"That sounds like a plan." His mother smiled. "Where will you set up shop?"

"I haven't worked out all the details yet." As tempting as it was to throw Hayden under the bus and ask about the south barn now, he wouldn't do that. Acting like an adult meant adult conversations— not using his mother to guilt his older brother into instantly agreeing to his proposition. "But I'm getting there."

A loud thump had them all stiffening. That was when John realized Weston, Brynn and Mya weren't playing in the great room.

"Silence is never a good thing." Hayden shook his head and hurried from the kitchen.

"Yup." Kyle followed.

His mother chuckled. "Parenthood is nonstop." She shrugged. "Oh, I'd better check on the rolls." She turned, opening the oven and peering inside.

"Was that why you were asking about the shop?" Nat whispered, her blue eyes locking with his. "You're wanting to rent out Grampa Bear's shop?"

"No." He shook his head. "But I appreciate the offer." He winked.

Nat rolled her eyes, but she was smiling. "You hear your daddy?" She propped Leslie against her shoulder and started patting her little back. "He's trying to be funny again."

"Trying to be?" he asked. "Ouch."

Leslie burped.

"Now you know how she feels," Nat said, smiling. "Good job, little one."

And there it was. Her smile. The gentle timbre of her voice. Leslie pressed close. Worse, all the damnable influx of feelings and emotions he didn't know what to do with. A few things he did know: he wanted Nat, *and* he knew better than to want what he couldn't have. He knew better, but that didn't stop the wanting.

Chapter Fourteen

Nat stood on the wide wraparound porch of the Mitchell ranch house, leaning against the railing to take in the view. It had been a long day—but a good one. The little ones were all in the care of their parents, and now she, Jan and John were enjoying the sunset in relative peace. "I forgot how big the place is," she said, her gaze sweeping the horizon. "There's no end to it, is there?"

"It does feel that way, sitting out here." Jan looked up from her knitting. "I've had the good fortune to travel all over, and I can honestly say this is the prettiest view on earth."

Nat could believe it. She hadn't traveled—except for the ride in the back of the white CPS car that drove her from Austin to Grampa Bear's front porch. She'd been too worn out to take note of the view. "It's so...tranquil."

She glanced at Leslie, sound asleep in the bouncy seat beside Jan's rocking chair. Alpha was sound asleep, too, lying on his side, a canine fence curving around Leslie. The poor dog didn't care much for Leslie's tantrums, but he seemed to have figured out that she was now one of his people.

Leslie was a Mitchell. This was her home. This could be Leslie's childhood. Big family dinners. Playing with cousins. Surrounded by dogs and laughter and conversation and love. This *should* be Leslie's childhood.

"It hasn't changed." John stood, propped up against the pole next to her, his arms crossed over his wall-like chest. "There were times I'd close my eyes and picture this, right here." He shook his head.

"You know what they say—*there is no place like home*," Jan said, her knitting needles clacking away. "But I've always believed it's having the people you love around you that truly makes a home."

John turned Nat's way, his gaze steady upon her.

Jan kept on knitting. "What good is a house or a piece of land if there's no one to share it with?"

"I need to remember that." Nat meant to stop there, but the words seemed to keep coming of their own volition. "Since Grampa Bear died, I've held on to things more than I should. I miss him so much. I wanted to hold on to something real, something that was his. I guess that's why I'm struggling with this auction. Selling the things that he treasured most—"

"Oh, Natalie, honey." Jan stopped knitting. "There is not one thing on this earth that he treasured more than you."

John nodded, his eyes dark in the fading light.

"I know. Rationally, I do." But being rational had become a bit challenging since John had arrived on her front porch.

"Bear would be heartsick to know you've been left with this mess. Heartsick." Jan shook her head. "And he'd be the first one to tell you to sell each and every one of those motorcycles. Nothing can take your memories, Nat, and that's what you need to hold on to."

Nat nodded.

"Now that I've dispensed my daily dose of wisdom, I think I'll turn in." She yawned, covering her mouth. "Excuse me."

"No, it's late. It's been a long day, and I should be heading home." She smiled. "Dinner was delicious, really. Thank you so much."

"I haven't made a good pot roast in a while, so when John reminded me that it was your favorite, I knew I had to make it," Jan said cheerfully.

John had reminded his mother? Wait… When she'd called John, she'd already been making it. So why had John made it sound like his mother's invitation was a spur-of-the-moment thing? Obviously, there'd been nothing spontaneous about it. She glanced his way again, but this time John was staring out over the darkening sky, the muscle in his jaw working.

What was he thinking?

Jan stood. "Please don't be a stranger, Natalie. If we can help out, in any way, let me know. I have a bit of fundraising experience under my belt that I'd be happy to put to use on your behalf." She hugged Nat close. "Thank you for taking care of John." When she pulled back, there were tears in the older woman's eyes. "You've always taken good care of him."

"Mom," John said, sighing.

"Don't *Mom* me." Jan brushed him aside. "It's my prerogative to thank Natalie for always being so good to you. It can't be easy, I'm sure of that."

"Really?" But John was smiling.

"It's not," Nat agreed. "He's stubborn and temperamental." *And handsome and passionate, and he's an incredible kisser, and he smells fantastic—*

"You ready to go?" John cut in. "'Night, Mom." He kissed her cheek.

"You leave Leslie with me," Jan said. "That car seat can't help with her colic."

"Thanks, Mom." John kissed her cheek. "I won't be long."

"I won't worry if you are." Jan waved. "Be careful."

"Colic?" Nat asked as they walked to the truck.

"Is she okay? Have you taken her to the doctor? What is it?"

"It's a fancy term for extra gas bubbles that make a baby extra fussy at night." John opened the passenger door for her. "I read about it in this book I found in Leslie's car seat."

It took willpower not to linger, to stare up into the handsome face and…and what? *Bad idea.* She climbed up and nodded her thanks when he closed the door.

"'Stubborn and temperamental'?" John asked, once they were on the road to town.

Nat shrugged. "Are you going to argue with that assessment?"

"I'd like to think those aren't the only two qualities you see in me." He glanced her way. "What about *charming*? Or *amusing*? Or a *decent cook*?"

"Except for bacon and eggs." She shook her head.

"Yeah, yeah." He sighed. "Fine. Not a decent cook. *Strong*?"

"I'll give you *strong*." She hadn't needed to see him shirtless to know he was strong. And, his stubbornness was a testament to his internal strength, too. Not to mention what he'd been through to get those scars… John Mitchell was one of the strongest people she knew. "No denying that."

"*Stubborn* and *temperamental* and *strong*?" He

looked at her. "I should put that on my online-dating profile."

Nat turned wide eyes his way. "You have an online-dating profile?"

He paused, studying her. "Not yet." His eyes narrowed.

Was he serious? No. He was teasing. "Are you… um, getting one?" She had to smile then.

"What?" He sounded…offended. Really offended.

"Nothing," she said, trying not to sound as shocked as she felt. John and online dating? It just didn't fit. "You're not joking?"

John kept on glaring at her, his eyes narrowing further.

"Okay." She cleared her throat. "Shouldn't you keep your eyes on the road?" she asked, struggling not to laugh at how defensive he was about this.

He faced forward, staring out the front windshield.

Nat hummed a few lines of Whitesnake's "Here I Go Again" before she turned back to him. "How is it going? At home, I mean? With your family?" That's when she noticed his smile. "Why is this funny?"

"It's not." He tapped his fingers on the steering wheel. "You humming big-hair rock songs is."

"Whatever." She shrugged. "I haven't had any complaints."

"I wasn't complaining." He shook his head. "I was smiling."

She looked at him.

He looked at her, smiling.

She had no choice but to smile back. "Things are okay? At home?"

"Things are…fine." He shrugged and went back to looking out the front windshield.

"'Fine'?" She frowned. "Fine isn't good."

"You don't need to worry about me. You've done that enough." He sighed. "How about you let me worry about you for a while?"

"I'm fine, too." She sighed. "Don't worry on my account."

"Okay…we're both fine." He went back to tapping his fingers on the steering wheel. "The Bear's House looks good. Hadn't been there in a while."

"About eight years or so?" she asked, glancing his way.

"Sounds about right." He chuckled. "Eight years ago. I can tell you this is not where I thought I'd wind up. But then, things don't always work out the way you plan." He shrugged. "I can honestly say that I'm here because I am stubborn and temperamental—just like you said."

She winced. "Oh… I was teasing."

"You were right." He shook his head.

"What happened, John? You're here and you'd think that would be enough to stop my nightmares but it hasn't." She knew she was pushing, but she couldn't help it. Of all the questions that ate at her, this one was the worst.

"You have nightmares about me?"

"About you being in danger. Or being hurt. Of course, I worried—worry—about you," she admitted. "That can't be a surprise. You're…you."

His gaze swept over her face before he said, "It won't surprise you to know that it all started with my smart mouth. My commanding officer and I didn't get along. I let him know it when he messed up. He didn't like it. Not that it stopped me." He sighed. "This time I'd pushed him a little too far, and he'd sent me to the discipline barracks to wait, alone, for my punishment. The base got bombed and me along with it. I was pinned, and I knew my leg wasn't right. It took time before they realized I was missing. By then, the knee was pretty much a loss." He didn't say anything for the rest of the drive.

But Nat couldn't get over what he'd told her. She'd had that dream—more than once. He'd been alone. How long had he been alone? He'd have been scared, of course he would have been. But this wasn't a dream. This really happened to him.

John pulled into Bear's driveway and turned off the ignition.

He turned to look at her then, the cab of the truck too dark for her to see him clearly.

"If you're making a face at me, I can't tell." Why was she so breathless?

"I'm not." His voice was low. With a click, the inside cab lights came on.

Her gaze got instantly tangled up with his. *It was better in the dark.* "Do you want to come inside?" she asked.

"No." He shook his head. "I don't think that's a good idea."

"Why not?" She didn't mean to sound snippy but…she did.

"Because of what happened last time I was here." The corner of his mouth cocked, and his gaze fell to her mouth, leaving no room for misunderstanding.

Nat's chest deflated, going warm and tingly. "It's not like we can't control ourselves." She drew in a deep breath, willing her brain not to go down memory lane… Now was not the time to think about how warm and smooth his skin had been beneath her touch. Her cheeks were burning. "That was a fluke." She wasn't sure who she was talking to: John or herself. "We were both lonely, that's all. Wanting companionship. But now we know better, and neither of us want…*that* to happen again."

"I'll have to respectfully disagree with you there, Nat." He cleared his throat. "So, it's probably best if I say good-night here."

Nat stared at him, in shock.

"If you keep looking at me like that, I'll be hard-pressed not to kiss you." The words were gruff. "What happens then?"

They both knew the answer to that. She ached just thinking about it.

"Go inside, Nat. I'm begging you." His hands tightened on the steering wheel. "I'm trying to be a good guy—to make the right choices." He cleared his throat. "Adult choices." The rasp in his voice made her shudder. "Responsible choices." He shook his head. "I don't want to do something we'll both regret. I don't want to mess things up. Like you said, you're…you."

It was as effective as a bucket of cold water. Regret. He'd regret kissing her… That was good. That was honest. He *wanted* her, but he didn't want *her*.

"Thanks for the help with the pictures. And for dinner." She opened the passenger door. "I had a nice time." She climbed out of the truck, hurried down the path to the house and closed the front door behind her. Why was she so upset? He threw back the words she'd used. He'd listened and was respecting what she'd said. She should be proud of him, not disappointed. And she was proud of him…but that didn't do a thing to ease the ache she had for him.

"Start the truck." He sat, staring at the closed front door. "Go home." But he couldn't move. He was on fire for Nat. It had nothing to do with being lonely or wanting companionship, and everything to do with wanting Nat. *Only Nat.*

"Dammit." He rested his forehead on the steering wheel. It was getting harder to ignore the truth about his feelings for Nat. "Nope." He shook his head and started the ignition, shutting down that line of thought. *Not going there.*

He drove home, music blaring, singing along— doing his best to shut down any thoughts of Nat and feelings and things he shouldn't be thinking about. When he parked in front of the house, most of the lights were off.

Good. Peace and quiet. He opened the front door. *Banshee Baby must be sleeping.* He grinned and headed into the kitchen, on the hunt for any leftovers. But when he clicked on the kitchen light, Hayden was standing there—holding the pan with the leftover pot roast.

John paused. He could be an ass and walk away, or he could try this adult thing and see what happened. *Why not?* "Looks like you beat me to it." He nodded at the tray of food.

"There's plenty." Hayden slid the tray on the marble countertop.

John nodded, pulling two plates from the cabinet.

"Thanks." Hayden took the plate John offered. "So…"

"Yeah." John nodded. "So." *Aw, hell. I'm not ready for this.* He turned his attention to fixing himself a plate.

Hayden did the same, the two of them taking turns microwaving their food, before sitting at the oversize kitchen table.

"Think Nat's going to come out okay?" Hayden asked. "Damn shame what she's having to deal with."

"Damn shame," he agreed. They had that much in common. "Harry seems to think the bikes will bring in more than enough. I know it's gutting her to do it, but it just makes sense." He shook his head. "I'm hoping she can hold on to the BMW. That's the one that has shared memories tied to it—when she and Bear would go riding together." He had memories of that one, too. He could remember Nat's braids sticking out from her too-big helmet, blowing straight back as Bear cruised down Main Street. "But it's also the one Harry said will bring in the most money."

Hayden nodded.

There was no point in delaying the conversation about the barn. No kids, no wives, no mother—no distractions. *Now is as good a time as any.* He took a deep breath and started. "I wanted to talk to you about using the south barn."

"What sort of renovations need to be made for it to be usable?" Hayden looked at him. "You'll have Bear's tools, but I'm guessing there might be some gaps that'll need to be filled."

John sat back in his chair. "You're okay with it?"

Hayden put his fork down. "Why wouldn't I be? This is your home just as much as it's mine and Kyle's."

John looked at his brother, trying to find the words to explain. "It doesn't feel like it. But I've been gone awhile." He broke off.

Hayden nodded. "Too long."

They stared at each other until the air between them was thick with tension. He knew he had a lot to apologize for, but it wasn't easy.

"I know you and I have things to work through, but you're my brother. I can't go back and change what happened but…if I could, I would." Hayden's gaze never wavered.

John ran a hand over his face. "You were doing what you thought was right." He stopped. "No, hell, you were doing what was right. I was being…a stubborn, temperamental, pain in the ass of a teenager." He swallowed.

"I should have taken it easy on you. The harder I pushed, the further I pushed you away." Hayden's voice was tight and gruff—revealing this was no easier for him than it was for John. "I had no business telling you what to do."

"You're my big brother, Hayden. Our father was

dead, and you saw our stepfather for the bastard he was." It was hard to say because it was all true. Every single time Hayden had tried to step in, to be the parent he and Kyle had needed, they'd dug in and made it worse. They'd preferred Ed's hands-off, freewill approach to Hayden reminding them to do their chores and think about how their behavior was affecting their mother. Hayden had done what needed to be done. "I was angry with the world, but I took it out on you. Leaving seemed like an escape." He snorted. "It wasn't."

Hayden frowned, his head snapping up. "You wouldn't have left if I'd given you some space." His gaze fell to John's leg. "You leaving and getting hurt, that's on me."

John could only stare now. Did Hayden really believe that? It wasn't true. He'd brought all of this on himself. Hayden needed to know that. "You told me once that I was on a path of self-destruction and I needed to change course before it was too late. Do you remember that?" He waited for Hayden to nod. "I was so cocksure of myself that I took that as a dare, even though you were right. Nothing you said or did could have stopped me from doing and saying and believing what I wanted to. This—" he paused, rubbing his left leg "—is karma. I did this all on my own. I'm lucky. You know it, and I know it."

They went back to staring. But this time, without the tension.

"I'm sorry," John said. "For all of it. We've lost too many years."

"I'm sorry, too." Hayden nodded. "But we have time now. As far as the barn goes, it's yours. I want you to feel like this is home again."

"I appreciate that." He'd been expecting yelling, more a fight than a civilized conversation. Learning that his big brother was just as remorseful and haunted by their past as he was gutted him. How much time had they wasted? Correction. How much time had *he* wasted? He was the one who went into every situation with his back up, braced and ready to take on whatever came his way. *I'm tired of fighting.* Especially when there wasn't a fight to be had.

"Can I ask a question?" Hayden pushed his now-empty plate back on the table. "About Leslie?"

John nodded.

"Is her mother coming back for her?" Hayden was watching him closely.

John shook his head. "She sent me a packet of papers. Leslie is mine, if I want her. But she also enclosed adoption forms..."

Hayden's jaw muscle clenched. "Is that what you're thinking?"

John pinched the bridge of his nose. "If you'd asked me that question ten days ago, I'd have said yes. I'm no more qualified to be a father than I am to be a brain surgeon. In both situations, messing up can lead to serious consequences."

"Isn't that the truth?" Hayden smiled. "What changed your mind?"

"Nat." He shrugged. "She just… She had a hard start, before she wound up with Bear. And something about her with Leslie made me… I don't know." He shrugged again. "She made it seem possible. Like, maybe I could do this—and that the family would welcome her."

"Did you doubt that?" Hayden frowned.

"I doubted every damn thing, Hayden." He ran a hand over his face. "When I got here, I was a mess. I put down roots in her couch, drank beer and wallowed in self-pity. Nat put up with it. All of it. Leslie showed up, and she went from taking care of one whiny, pathetic individual to two. And I'm nowhere near as cute as Leslie." He grinned.

Hayden chuckled. "She is cute."

"And so damn tiny." John shook his head. "I've never seen anyone that tiny before."

"Weston was premature." Hayden nodded. "The first time I held him, I was convinced I'd break him."

John shuddered at the thought of holding a baby even smaller than Leslie. "Nope. Couldn't do it."

Hayden chuckled again. "So what happened? Nat wouldn't just kick you out without a reason."

"She had plenty of reason before Emily's letter showed up. But once the letter arrived, that did it. She couldn't fathom me giving Leslie up. She was disappointed in me, said I was making excuses and I needed to stop being so damn selfish and grow up." He sighed. "She was right, of course, on all counts."

"And she kicked you out?" Hayden was watching him.

"She did." He met his brother's gaze. "And I've been missing her pretty much every damn day since I left."

"Because she's your best friend?" Hayden's brows rose. "I think you've said that a good dozen times now. I'm just waiting to see how many times it takes before you face facts."

"Facts?" There was no misunderstanding what his brother was getting at. "Like how she deserves better."

"You'll be fine with her falling in love, getting hitched and having a family with someone else?" Hayden asked.

"Who?" He frowned. "She didn't mention anyone when I was staying with her." If she was involved with someone, she'd never have let things progress between them the way they had. Not Nat. She was too true-blue for that. Still, the idea bothered him. Not just a little but a whole hell of a lot.

"That's what I thought." Hayden smiled. "You've

got something worth fighting for, John. So fight. If you think she deserves better, do better."

Nat's ultimatum had given him the drive to do just that. Do better. Be better. Even if he did face facts and admit he loved Nat far more than he'd imagined possible, that didn't mean she'd love him back. She'd said she'd loved him once... Maybe Hayden was right. Maybe now was the time to fight. He'd never be good enough for her, but he'd never stop trying. Because this was Nat... And he loved her.

Chapter Fifteen

Nat turned the key again. Nothing. No click. No grind. Silence. She bit into her bottom lip, on the verge of tears. She'd already scalded her hand with coffee, torn a hole along the seam of her jeans and had a headache. Now this? The auction started in two hours. Even though Harry had assured her there was no reason for her to be there, she wanted to be: she needed to see this through. If Grampa Bear's old truck didn't start, she wasn't going anywhere. She couldn't get it going, but she knew someone who could.

She climbed out of the vehicle, slammed the door and headed inside. No matter how hard she tried to stay away from John, the universe seemed to conspire against her. In the week since she'd had dinner with the Mitchells, she'd gone back to dodging his calls, and he'd left daily messages with Leslie updates. Walt said he'd come into the bar twice, hung out long enough to see if she was working, then left—but he hadn't come by the house. She just couldn't trust herself not to get closer to him, and she wasn't ready. Or maybe she was afraid he wasn't ready.

She dialed, and rings barely started when John answered.

"Nat?" He sounded concerned.

Her heart lurched. *I don't have the time for this.* "My truck won't start. I need a mechanic."

"On my way." He hung up.

She stared at the phone. "Thank you," she murmured, replacing the phone on the cradle.

He was there fifteen minutes later.

"How fast were you going?" she asked, shielding her eyes from the rising sun.

"I'm here." He tipped his straw cowboy hat back on his head. "The auction's today, isn't it? You need to get there." He was already peering under the open hood of the ancient truck.

She held her breath, waiting...

"How about I give you a ride?" he asked, shaking his head and pointing at the truck. "That's not a quick fix."

"I can't ask you to do that." She managed to smile. "Thank you, though."

"Nat." He sighed. "You want to be there, don't you?"

"Harry said they don't need me—"

"But you want to go?" He paused, his hands on his hips. "Otherwise, you wouldn't have called me over here to fix the truck."

He had her there.

"Let's go." He nodded at the truck.

She should tell him no. But…she did want to be there. Only one thing made her hesitate. "What about Leslie?"

"I'll call." He held the door open for her.

Nat climbed in, watching as he walked around the hood of the truck. In his pale blue plaid button-up shirt, weathered jeans and straw hat, John Mitchell looked every bit the cowboy. When he slid into his seat and gave her a wink, Nat almost laughed… But she wasn't fully recovered from the image he cut in those jeans.

He started the truck, pulled out onto the road and pressed a button on the dashboard. The sound of a ringtone filled the cab.

"Mitchell residence." It was Jan.

"Mom, Nat's truck broke down." John glanced over his shoulder for oncoming traffic, then pulled out onto the highway, Austin-bound.

"Oh, no." His mother's distress was almost comical. "Isn't the auction today? You should take her, John. She needs to be there—to have closure."

Nat stared out the passenger window. Closure would be nice. With any luck the whole IRS debacle would be over and done with today.

"You've got Leslie?" John asked.

"Hayden and Kyle took their families to Fredericksburg for the rodeo, so don't you fret over a thing. It's just me and my granddaughter."

Nat glanced at John.

"I appreciate it, Mom," John said, smiling.

"Be safe driving, and give Nat my love. Bye, now." The phone cut off.

"She doesn't get the speakerphone concept." John shook his head. "Any other objections?" His gaze bounced her way.

Nat shook her head, avoiding his gaze. "Thank you, John. Really."

"You look tired, Nat."

From the corner of her eye, she saw him reach for her, then stop himself.

"Not sleeping?"

Not much. She'd had two phone calls with her IRS counselor, and neither had gone well. She needed today to be a success. "A lot on my mind." She tried to shrug him off.

"It's almost an hour drive. Try to get some sleep." This time his hand rested on hers—right on top of her burn.

She winced and pulled away from him. "Maybe I will try." At the very least, she could pretend she was sleeping. John was being nothing but helpful. It wasn't his fault that she was wound up so tight. He had nothing to do with any of this… He might have had a little to do with her sleeplessness. It was always one of two scenarios. He was either getting shot at or blown up or in imminent danger, or he was doing all sorts of incredible things to her with his hands and mouth and body. All the things she'd imagined them doing countless times.

She woke up an hour later.

"We're here." John smiled at her. "You ready for this?"

"Yes." *No.*

An hour later, three of the six she'd agreed to sell had been purchased well under Harry's estimate, and she was feeling more than a little disheartened. The other two bikes sold for even lower. So far, she'd cleared a hundred and thirty thousand dollars for all five. *Not enough.*

"Not too bad," John murmured. "The Scout's sure to bring in the money."

Nat nodded. She'd waffled about selling the 1929 classic, but she had no choice. Still, seeing it wheeled up onto the revolving dais in the room full of people put a knot in her throat. When the numbers started flying and the bidders' paddles started rising, she reached for John's hand. There was something immediately grounding about his touch.

"Do I hear forty thousand dollars?" the auctioneer called out.

There was a momentary stall.

"John," she whispered. "That's forty-one thousand dollars I still owe."

But a paddle went up, John squeezed her hand, and she started breathing again.

"Going, going…" The auctioneer whacked the podium. "Sold for forty-nine thousand dollars."

Thirty-two thousand dollars.

She didn't remember John leading her back to the truck or the drive to get burgers or when they left Austin city limits. All she could think about was how she was going to come up with thirty-two thousand dollars. Maybe she could rent out the shop? But that wouldn't get her the money now. And she needed it now. She'd already talked to the bank, and the interest rates they'd offered would make her pay back almost double what she owed by the time she was done with a loan.

"You good?" John asked, still holding her hand. "It's going to be okay."

"How?" she asked, staring down at their joined hands. "How is this going to be okay?" She shook her head and pulled her hand free, glancing at the cheerful *Welcome to Granite Falls* sign.

"We'll figure it out, Nat," he murmured, softly.

"We?" Her voice wavered.

"Yes, we," he said, more firmly this time.

"I appreciate your help today, John. I do." She hated how unsteady she sounded. "But this is something I have to take care of."

"Let me help." The words were edged with frustration.

She didn't answer. Today had been one colossal disappointment. Without the full amount, she felt no better off than she'd been before she'd sold off Grampa Bear's treasured motorcycles. She was angry and sad and overwhelmed and...hopeless. That was the worst of it. She only had one option now. And it hurt her heart to think of giving it up.

Tears were coming—she felt it. After the day she'd had, she couldn't bear crying in front of anyone. Even though no one at today's auction knew a thing about her situation, there'd been an element of humiliation to it all. Selling family heirlooms to the highest bidder? Not something she was proud of. If she broke down and sobbed uncontrollably in front of an audience, it would be more than she could take.

She was already reaching for the door handle when he pulled into Bear's driveway. "Thank you for today. You're right. It will be fine." She was out of the truck and running to the front door, her cheeks already wet with tears.

John parked the truck, ran a hand over his face and climbed out. He didn't care if she slammed the door in his face, he wasn't leaving her like this. Today had been heartbreaking, he knew that. He'd watched her face as, little by little, the hope faded away.

And dammit all, he didn't know what to do about it.

But leaving her? Now? That wasn't an option.

Vlad was in the hammock swing, leaning forward and staring at the closed front door with his one good eye.

"I'll check on her," he said. *When the hell had talking to a raccoon become the norm?* He knocked. "Nat?"

No answer.

"Nat, please let me in." He knocked again.

Still no answer.

He sighed. "Do I go in?" He glanced at Vlad. *Am I asking a frigging raccoon for advice?* He shook his head and turned the doorknob. *Of course.* The door swung wide. Now probably wasn't the time to bring up locking the front door...

He walked inside. "Nat?"

She wasn't in the kitchen or the living room.

"Nat?" he called out, walking down the hallway.

Bear's bedroom door was open, so he peered inside. Old polaroid pictures, legal papers, newspaper clippings, Nat's school pictures and some handwritten letters covered Bear's massive bed. Nat, reminiscing? What did she have left except her memories, this house and the Bear's House? *She has every right to be upset.*

Hell, he'd been so worried about her he'd had a hard time keeping calm.

"Nat?" he called out again. He left Bear's room and walked to the end of the hall.

Her bedroom was empty.

But he heard the shower, and he heard Nat. She was sobbing. Not the silent tears she'd denied existed but the tears of grief. Something had broken inside of her, he heard it. It reached inside his chest, wrapped barbwire around his heart and pulled the wire tight. *Oh, Nat. I'm so sorry.*

He leaned against the wall to wait. If she needed him, he was here. But for now, she needed to cry it out. There was nothing wrong with that. She'd more than earned it. But the shower stayed on, and there was no easing Nat's tears.

He knocked on the door. "Nat?"

The sobbing stopped. "John?"

"It's just me." He pressed his hand against the door. "I couldn't leave."

"I'm…fine." But her voice was shaking and a telltale sob reached him.

"I'm coming in." He turned the knob.

She was insistent. "I'm f-fine."

He wasn't sure what he'd expected to find, but this wasn't it. She sat, her arms wrapped around her knees, in the corner of the bathtub with the shower head turned against the wall. Rivulets of water streamed down her back and head, making her hair into a slick cap. He didn't care that she was naked, he cared that she was hurting.

The anguish and exhaustion on her face about did him in.

He crouched and turned off the ice-cold water. "You're going to make yourself sick."

"That's an old wives' tale," she sniffed. "You can't get sick from cold water."

"I don't know, Nat, that's pretty damn cold."

"The hot water ran out." Her eyes were blood-shot, her nose was red and swollen, and she seemed to droop—all of her—in defeat.

"Come on." He stood and grabbed the thick white towel from the rack.

She shook her head.

"Nat." He held out the towel. "I won't look."

She rested her forehead on her knees. "It's not that." She shivered.

He draped the towel around her shoulders. "What?"

"I'm feeling a little woozy," she admitted, peeking at him from under her arm.

She hadn't touched the burger and fries he'd bought her. "What have you eaten today?"

She shrugged.

"Anything?" he asked.

She shrugged again.

"Then, you need to eat something." He reached for her.

"I'm not hungry—"

"Nat." He smoothed the hair from her face.

"You're not taking care of yourself. You took care of me. Let me take care of you." His voice lowered.

She nodded and stood, using the towel as a shield, and took his hand to step from the tub. "Thank you." And then she was crying all over again.

John scooped her up in his arms. "I've got you." He carried her into the living room and sat in Bear's oversize recliner.

She sobbed so hard the chair was shaking. He wasn't sure what to say. He didn't want to offer up false reassurances, but he couldn't say nothing. "I'm so sorry, Nat." He drew in a deep breath, rubbing his hand along her back.

"I'm losing everything," she whispered.

His breath caught. "No. You're not."

"I am, John," she sniffed. "You don't… You can't understand."

"Then, tell me. I want to." He buried his nose in her damp hair.

Her breathing evened out slowly. "I don't know who my father is, and my mother was…my mother wasn't a good person." She swallowed. "I learned to cook when I was six. Macaroni and cheese. Noodle soup. Nothing fancy, but enough to keep myself and my mom fed. And whichever guy she'd brought home. I figured out how to squeeze into the water-heater closet to hide when things got bad, and I woke up on a stranger's couch more than once—with no idea how I got there or where my mom was."

John's hold on her tightened. He'd known it was bad, but this? Picturing her hiding? Waking up alone and afraid?

"I don't know who called CPS, but I wish I did. I'd thank them." Her breath wavered. "Do you think CPS tells them? When they do something good or save a kid, does CPS give them any sort of reassurance?"

"I don't know, Nat." He sounded gruff.

"Grampa Bear said they couldn't due to privacy issues." She sighed, her head heavy against his shoulder. "But I like to pretend they know. And that they know I'm grateful because they changed my whole life."

He nodded. As far as he was concerned, they were real-life superheroes.

"Did you know Grampa Bear was the first man to hug me? He called me by my name and treated me like an equal. He never got impatient with me or tried to shove me into a dress or sided against me—even when I'd done wrong." She shook her head. "He was my champion. My hero. My whole family. The only one I could rely on." Her voice broke. "He's gone, John. My family is gone."

He hugged her closer. *You can rely on me. I'm here*. But he knew now wasn't the time to tell her how he felt. Right now, she needed someone to listen and be there for her. That someone was him.

"Today I watched bits of him being sold. The Scout was something he'd worked on with his father. His Honda Super Hawk was the first bike he'd raced—and crashed. He'd rebuilt it himself. Six bikes. Six stories. Six treasures that he'd held on to because they meant something to him. And I sold them." She pushed out of his lap, gripping her towel in place.

He was up. "Nat—"

She held her hand out, silencing him. "No, John, listen. You have a big, loving family. You might not always see eye to eye, but you know, without a doubt, they'd do anything for you. They'd defend you and support you and love you, no matter what you did." She looked up at him. "Do you know how lucky you are? Really?"

He didn't. Not really.

"It hurts me to see you give up on life. To choose bitterness or watch you hold on to your anger and keep yourself apart from them rather than see the part you've played in things." She shook her head. "I'm fighting to hold on to something that ties me to my only family member. He was it. He's gone. I'm alone." She could barely look his way. "Again."

"Dammit, Nat, I'm here." He reached for her. "Let me be here."

She stared up at him then, her eyes a startling

blue. "You can't be here for your own daughter. Why should I believe you'll be here for me?" She covered her mouth with her hand.

He stepped back, her words landing body blows. "Test me all you want. I'm not going anywhere."

"Test you?" She frowned. "I don't need to test you, John. I know you. You should go. I'm tired and sad and angry and bound to say something else I'll regret." She shook her head. "Please, just go." She walked down the hall to her room and closed the door behind her.

He was pretty sure there wasn't much else she could say. Nat was hurting. He knew what it was like to be consumed with hurt and grief. It was a dark place, one that was hard to escape. She was lashing out, what else could she do? He might not understand her childhood or the wounds it had left, but he understood this.

She'd never deserted him, no matter how hard he'd pushed back. *I won't let you down.*

He stayed long enough to make some soup, put it in the microwave for later and clean up the kitchen. He wrote a quick note and knocked on Nat's door, but she was sound asleep when he peeked inside. He propped it on her side table and crept out, closing the door carefully. He was on his way out when he went into Bear's room. So many pictures. So many memories. Nat in the side-car and Bear on the bike, both grinning like kids.

Nat, in braids and covered in grease, holding a wrench at the ready, while Bear wiped his hands on a shop towel, laughing. The two of them fishing. A picture of Nat after the school play holding flowers, and Bear beaming with pride at her side. Good memories for Nat to hold on to and display. The perfect way to help her hold on to her grandfather and the love he had for her. He collected several of the pics he knew would mean the most and wrapped them in a handkerchief. It would never erase her loss, but it might ease the hole left behind.

Chapter Sixteen

"Careful," Nat said, hugging herself as the two men rolled the 1943 BMW R75 military motorcycle and sidecar combo into the waiting towing trailer. The bike shifted to the right, the front wheel spinning back, and making her repeat, "Careful."

"Yes, ma'am. We got it." One of them was all smiles. She couldn't tell if he was hitting on her or if he'd picked up on how fragile she was and was doing his best to make this as painless as possible.

The other one sighed, muttered something under his breath and had no problem letting her know that he had zero need or tolerance for input.

Right back at you. She hugged herself tighter. "Did you get the cover?" she asked. "It was custom-made for the bike."

The smiling one nodded. "Yes, ma'am. We'll use it and cover it with a padded tarp. Nice and safe for transport."

The other one shot her the side-eye.

"Good," she said, resisting the urge to say something snarky to the one with the bad attitude.

The roar of an engine told her John and his brothers were here. She'd called Jan and asked her to relay the message, asking John to come over before she went to work—too horrified by what she'd said to him to talk to him directly. She'd been horrible, lashing out at him when he was doing everything he could to offer her comfort.

Instead of storming out, he'd left her soup, a note to get some sleep and to call him—in case she needed him. *I need you, John.* But needing him was asking too much of him. How could she rely on him, ask him to be there for her, when he was only now finding his way?

I can't.

All she could do was apologize for her cruelty and get this over with. The bike. The tools. *Over and done with.* She glanced back over her shoulder, searching for John.

"Nat." Hayden waved.

"Hi." She tried to infuse some sense of welcome, but at this point, she'd shoot for being civil.

"What's happening here?" Kyle asked.

"Buyer." She swallowed. Thanks to Harry, a private buyer had reached out to her with an offer she couldn't refuse. This sale, plus the auction, had done it. She'd made the money she needed. And left some. *The answer to my prayers.* How could she refuse? "They're here to pick it up and deliver it." She rubbed her hands up and down her arms.

"That was fast." John joined them, his straw cowboy hat casting half his face in shadow.

She nodded, doing her best not to stare or beg for his forgiveness right here and now. Had he been right? Had she been testing him? There was only one thing she was certain of. Three days ago she'd humiliated herself, naked and sobbing and pathetic, and said unforgettably cruel things.

"That's good?" Kyle asked.

She nodded. "Great." She sounded anything *but* great, and the Mitchell brothers noticed. She kept right on going, her nerves on edge. "The shop is unlocked. If you want to back up, it might be easier."

"Sounds good." John nodded, an air of enthusiasm about him Nat hadn't seen in some time.

"You're excited about this?" she said.

"About becoming a contributing member of society?" He shrugged. "I'll miss the all-day Clint Eastwood marathons, sure, but they do sort of run together after a while."

"After a while?" Nat shook her head. "Try one."

"Not a fan?" Kyle asked.

She shook her head. "I don't see what all the hype is about."

"Says the woman who can recite all the lyrics to Aerosmith's 'Cryin'?' I still haven't quite figured you out." But John was smiling.

Did that mean he didn't hate her for being so

awful to him when he was here last? *Please don't hate me.*

"Nat." John's hand settled on her upper arm, leaving an instant and alarming tingle. "I had to bring Leslie. Mom is—"

"Leslie's here?" She peered around him. "Where is she?"

"Sleeping." John headed toward the truck so she followed. "You sure you don't mind keeping an eye on her while we load everything up?"

"I'm sure." If there was anything that could make today better, it was Leslie. That, and hoping John would forgive her. "I'm glad you brought her."

His gaze was warm. "I'd hoped you'd feel that way."

"Of course I do. You know I love her." She swallowed. "I'll always take Leslie cuddles." She watched him pull the infant car seat from the truck. "How is her colic?"

He shrugged. "It's giving her plenty of opportunity to practice her banshee wail."

Nat smiled in spite of herself.

He carried the car seat and diaper bag inside and set them both on the floor. "We'll try to get out of your hair."

"No rush." She glanced at him, feeling oddly shy. "Is it okay if I take her out?"

He nodded, looking perplexed. "You need to ask?"

"It's been a while since you two lived here—"

"A few weeks," John said.

She nodded, surprised at how quickly he'd answered. Had it only been a few weeks? It seemed like more. Each and every one of them more miserable than the last.

"You don't need to ask, Nat." He stepped forward.

"I'm so sorry, John." She swallowed. "For what I said to you. Please forgive me. I was—"

"It'd been a hell of a day. A bad day. But thank you for the apology." He took her hand and gave it a quick squeeze.

She nodded again, the knot of guilt that had been crushing her chest fading away.

"I know you've got a lot going on, but I was hoping you could make a little time for me."

"For what?" There was something odd about his expression—something that tripped an alarm bell.

"To talk." He glanced at Leslie. "I've made some decisions that might affect you."

And just like that, ice-cold panic crashed into her. Leslie? What else could it be? "I don't think I'm up for it." She turned, unbuckling Leslie and lifting her slight weight into her arms. "I'm feeling a little…emotionally bruised." She closed her eyes and rested her cheek against the top of Leslie's head. "Can it wait?" She didn't look at him or open her eyes; she was too scared of what she'd see on his face.

"It can wait." The tenderness in his voice was too much to ignore.

Her eyes opened. His face, his beautiful face. She'd loved him for so long, she couldn't imagine stopping now. Whatever he'd decided, she had to trust he'd thought things through.

"If that's what you need." He shoved his hands into his pockets. "You look tired, Nat."

She shrugged. *I am tired.*

"You sure this is okay?" he asked. "You watching Leslie?"

"I'm certain." She carried Leslie to the recliner. "Will she need a bottle?"

"In an hour or so. We'll try to finish before that."

"Like I said, no rush." Now that Leslie was in her arms, the world felt a little brighter. "How are you, little one?" she asked. "You've gotten even bigger since I saw you last."

Leslie wriggled and squirmed, her long-lashed eyes opening and fixing on her face.

"Well, hello." Nat smiled. "Who's the prettiest baby in the whole wide world? Do you know?" She paused. "I do. It's you."

Leslie squeaked and stretched.

"I've missed you," she whispered, hating the sting in her eyes.

"Nat." John's voice was low. "Did you get what you needed? For the bike?"

"More than enough." She nodded. "Harry didn't disappoint. I only wish he'd found this collector before all the others were sold."

"I'm sorry it came to this." He glanced back and forth between her and Leslie. "If I'd had the money—"

"I wouldn't have taken it." She sighed, turning her attention back to Leslie. "You know that."

"It wouldn't stop me from trying." He smiled. "But *you* know that." He nodded, then left, the front door slamming behind him. "Hey, Vlad. How's it going?" His voice faded.

"You know something, Leslie?" she asked the baby. "I think Vlad misses your daddy and Alpha. I know Vlad misses Alpha's dog food." She smiled.

Leslie blinked, her little eyes intent and focused.

"Look at you, all wide-eyed and alert." She sighed, propping Leslie on her lap, facing her, and taking one little fist in each of her hands. "I'll tell you a secret, Leslie. Vlad isn't the only one missing you and your daddy. I do, too." She smiled at Leslie's open-mouthed yawn. "Let's hope your daddy will be more excited to hear that." Whatever decision John made, it wouldn't change the way she felt about him. She was proud of the strides he was making to get himself on track. He was capable of so much more than he gave himself credit for. She wanted to say as much… And that she loved him. Because she did, so much. And maybe, since he'd made her soup and forgiven her, he could love her, too.

John had waited two days to get here. No matter how hard he begged, his brothers hadn't let him out of their sights. They'd even hidden his truck keys. He knew they meant well, but it'd pissed him off. He hadn't wanted to wait this long to talk to Nat. A few cuts and bruises were no big deal—no matter what the doctor had said.

Now, finally, he was here. Nervous as hell and just as determined. He pushed open the front door of the Bear's House, a box tucked under his arm. The room was empty, except for Nat. She was wiping down the bar. "It's almost closing time," she called out, not bothering to look.

"I'm waiting for someone meeting me after work," he said, making his way to the bar.

"John?" Nat looked up at him, surprised. "What are you—" She broke off, her eyes going round. "What happened to your face?"

"Fell off a horse." He shrugged and sat. And his face looked exactly like he felt, battered and bruised and sore as hell.

Nat blinked. "You fell off a horse?"

"But on the fourth time, I stayed on." He

grinned. It had been a long time since he'd felt that sort of victory. "I might be banged up, but I earned every damn scratch and bruise." He shrugged. "Still working out the best angle for a saddle attachment but Dougal McCarrick thinks he can fashion something that'll help my leg. You know how good his leatherwork is."

"I do." She nodded. "I'm… Wow… It looks like it really hurts but…good for you."

"I had to wait to get the all clear to drive." He shrugged. "Doctors and their concussion protocols."

"You…you got a concussion? Wait. What?" She threw her towel on the counter. "Why didn't anyone call me?"

He propped an elbow on the counter. "Pretty sure I had enough people trying to take care of me."

Nat crossed her arms over her chest. "Who are you waiting for?"

He glanced at the clock. "They'll be finished up and here any minute." He sat the box on the bar. "How about some music?" He headed to the jukebox, clicked on "Carry On My Wayward Son" by Kansas and headed back to his seat. "You know this one, I think?"

Nat rolled her eyes.

"I think I caught Leslie humming it the other day." He sighed.

Nat was laughing then. "She'll grow up with great taste in music."

"Guess we'll have to wait and see." He tapped his fingers on the box.

Deep lines formed between Nat's brows as she pushed the swinging saloon doors into the kitchen and returned with a tub full of clean dishes. Her movements were a little jerky, almost agitated, when she started stacking the glasses.

He saw her glance at the door, twice, and couldn't help but grin.

The song ended and "Pour Some Sugar on Me" by Def Leppard came on.

She shot him a look. "So far, I approve of this playlist." She finished putting the glasses away and looked at the clock. "Whoever you're waiting for, I'm locking the door. You'll have to reschedule because I'm tired."

"Technically, the person I was waiting for is already here."

"Me?" Nat sighed, but she was smiling. "You think you're being funny again, don't you?"

He nodded, watching as she walked across and locked the front door. "Does this mean you're off the clock?" Why the hell was he so nervous all of a sudden? He knew she could laugh in his face. But there was also the chance that she felt something for him, too.

"Technically, I'm never off the clock." She shrugged. "The perks of owning the place."

"It's got to feel good to say that. Now that you've got the money to pay everything off."

"I won't breathe easy until I get my free-and-clear letter from the IRS." She took off her black apron and hung it on a hook on the back wall. "They said it could take four to six weeks."

"Since you're never off the clock, I guess I don't need to wait to talk to you." He took a deep breath. *This is going to be harder than I thought.* "Nat, I wanted to talk to you—"

"About the decisions you've made?" She hugged herself. "I remember. You said it would impact me?"

"I'll get to that part." He cleared his throat. "I've taken some time to figure things out and get my stuff straight. Sound familiar?"

She nodded, wary. "Vaguely."

"You know about the shop. I've hired on some folks to help get the place ready for business. Mitchell Garage will be open in under a month. I've got the permits for the mechanic shop. Now I'm looking into advertising. And I've got the tools." He smiled.

"I'm glad, John. You can do whatever you set your mind to."

"Having a job is part of being a responsible

grown-up, don't you think? It helps that I'm a kick-ass mechanic."

"And modest, too." She was smiling. "Did you take notes or something?"

"I have a good memory when it comes to important things." He paused, staring at her. "You've done a lot for me, Nat. More than you can ever know."

Her smile wavered. "That sounds a little ominous."

"Just wanted to make sure you got where I'm coming from." He pushed the box across the counter. "This is for you."

"Why?" She frowned.

"Why am I giving you a present?"

"Are you trying to tell me something? This feels a lot like goodbye."

"I'm giving you the present because I want to." He chuckled. "And I've no plans for any goodbyes."

Her brows rose, but she opened the box—and froze. A collage of photos. Bear and Nat. Working in the shop. Nat smiling in the sidecar. She and Bear wearing matching leather jackets. Smiles. Love. And happy memories.

"I know you miss him but you will never lose him, Nat. He'll always be in your heart, and now he'll be on your wall so you can see him whenever you want." He cleared his throat, hoping like hell this wouldn't backfire. The last thing he wanted to do was remind her of something painful. "Are they okay?"

She nodded. "They are more than okay, John." Her voice was thick. "This is incredible. I love them."

"There's one more, wrapped in paper." He pointed, and she picked up the single-framed picture, tearing away its covering. If he thought he was nervous before, he was damn near shaking in his boots now.

"What is…" Her eyes flew to his.

"I took that when you came to dinner. I wanted it, for myself." He swallowed, watching her face as he said, "Everything I want in the world is in that picture, Nat."

"This?" She held up the picture for him, her blue eyes meeting his.

"That." He nodded. It was Nat, smiling sweetly, with Leslie cradled close. "All I have to do is look at it and I'm happy."

She was still staring at him.

"I'm a work in progress, but I'll always put you and Leslie first, I promise." He stood, coming slowly around the bar. "I know damn good and well I'll never be good enough for you, but I'll never stop trying."

"John…" She shook her head.

"You can say no." He stopped moving. "But

I'm not giving up on you. Just like you've never given up on me. I want you to marry me. I want to be your family, Nat. Me and you and Leslie—"

She had her arms wrapped around his neck before he knew it. "And Alpha?"

He kissed her. "Even your damn raccoon."

She laughed.

His hands cradled her face. "I love you, Nat. I know that. I love you." He ran his knuckles along her cheek. "I want you." He smoothed her hair aside.

"I love you, too." She sighed. "I've loved you since the day you tripped Buzz Lafferty for pulling my braids."

"I've been a fool for that long?" He shook his head. "All that time wasted."

"That means we have a lot to make up for." Those blue eyes stared up at him as her hands slid down to rest on his chest.

"We do." He ran his nose along hers. "And we have a lot to look forward to." He kissed her slow and sweet. "I'm glad you didn't give up on me."

"I tried, so many times, but my heart wouldn't listen."

He pressed a hand over her heart. "It knew I'd come around and that, when I did, there was no one that could ever love you more than I do."

Her hands covered his, pressing his hand closer to her heart.

"I think my mother was right, Nat. The only time I really feel at home is when I'm with you." He kissed her forehead.

"Welcome home, John." She stood on tiptoe to kiss him.

"Nat…" He bent his head to kiss her. "There's no place like home."

* * * * *

WE HOPE YOU ENJOYED
THIS BOOK FROM

⟨H⟩ HARLEQUIN
SPECIAL
EDITION

Believe in love. Overcome obstacles. Find happiness.

Relate to finding comfort and strength in the
support of loved ones and enjoy the journey
no matter what life throws your way.

6 NEW BOOKS AVAILABLE EVERY MONTH!

#2887 A SOLDIER'S DARE
The Fortunes of Texas: The Wedding Gift • by Jo McNally

When Jack Radcliffe dares Belle Fortune to kiss him at the Hotel Fortune's Valentine's Ball, he thinks he's just having fun. She's interested in someone else. But from the moment their lips touch, the ex-military man is in trouble. The woman he shouldn't want challenges him to confront his painful past...and face his future head-on...

#2888 HER WYOMING VALENTINE WISH
Return to the Double C • by Allison Leigh

When Delia Templeton is tapped to run her wealthy grandmother's new charitable foundation, she finds herself dealing with Mac Jeffries, the stranger who gave her a bracing New Year's kiss. Working together gives Delia and Mac ample opportunity to butt heads...and revisit that first kiss as Valentine's Day fast approaches...

#2889 STARLIGHT AND THE SINGLE DAD
Welcome to Starlight • by Michelle Major

Relocating to the Cascade Mountains is the first step in Tessa Reynolds's plan to reinvent herself. Former military pilot Carson Campbell sees the bold and beautiful redhead only wreaking havoc with his own plan to be the father his young daughter needs. As her feelings for Carson deepen, Tessa finally knows who she wants to be—the woman who walks off with Carson's heart...

#2890 THE SHOE DIARIES
The Friendship Chronicles • by Darby Baham

From the outside, Reagan "Rae" Doucet has it all: a coveted career in Washington, DC, a tight circle of friends and a shoe closet to die for. When one of her crew falls ill, however, Rae is done playing it safe. The talented but unfulfilled writer makes a "risk list" to revamp her life. But forgiving her ex, Jake Saunders, might be one risk too many...

#2891 THE FIVE-DAY REUNION
Once Upon a Wedding • by Mona Shroff

Law student Anita Virani hasn't seen her ex-husband since the divorce. Now she's agreed to pretend she's still married to Nikhil until his sister's wedding celebrations are over—because her former mother-in-law neglected to tell her family of their split!

#2892 THE MARINE'S RELUCTANT RETURN
The Stirling Ranch • by Sabrina York

She'd been the girl he'd always loved—until she married his best friend. Now Crystal Stoker was a widowed single mom and Luke Stirling was trying his best to avoid her. That was proving impossible in their small town. The injured marine was just looking for a little peace and quiet, not expecting any second chances, especially ones he didn't dare accept.

YOU CAN FIND MORE INFORMATION ON UPCOMING HARLEQUIN TITLES, FREE EXCERPTS AND MORE AT HARLEQUIN.COM.

HSECNM0122A

"I won! I won!"

"That you did," he said, laughing and trying to climb out of his own tube. With his long legs, he was having a hard time getting out on his own, so I reached out my hand to help him up. As soon as he grabbed me, we both went soaring, feet away from the slides. I was amazed neither of us fell onto the ground, but I think just when we were about to, he caught me midair and steadied us.

"Okay, so a deal is a deal. Truth. Do you like me?"

"I can't believe you wasted your truth on something you already know."

"Maybe a girl needs to hear it sometimes."

"Reagan Doucet, I will tell you all day long how much I like you," he said, bending down again so he could stare directly into my eyes. "But you have to believe me when I do. No more of that 'c'mon, Jake' stuff. You either believe me or you don't."

"Deal," I said, grabbing hold of the loops on the waist of his pants to bring him even closer to me. "You got it."

"Mmm, no. I've got you," he whispered, bringing his lips centimeters away from mine but refusing to kiss me. Instead, he stood there, making me wait, and then flicked out his tongue with a grin, barely scraping the skin on my lips. It was clear Jake wanted me to want him. Better yet, crave him. And while I could also tell this was him putting on his charm armor again, I didn't care. I was in shoe, Christmas lights and sexy guy heaven, and for once I was determined to enjoy it. Not much could top that.

"Now, let's go find these pandas."

I reached out my hand, and he took it as we went skipping to the next exhibit.

Don't miss The Shoe Diaries *by Darby Baham,*
available February 2022 wherever
Harlequin Special Edition books and ebooks are sold.

Harlequin.com

HSEEXP0122A

Get 4 FREE REWARDS!

We'll send you 2 FREE Books plus 2 FREE Mystery Gifts.

Harlequin Special Edition books relate to finding comfort and strength in the support of loved ones and enjoying the journey no matter what life throws your way.

FREE
Value Over
$20

YES! Please send me 2 FREE Harlequin Special Edition novels and my 2 FREE gifts (gifts are worth about $10 retail). After receiving them, if I don't wish to receive any more books, I can return the shipping statement marked "cancel." If I don't cancel, I will receive 6 brand-new novels every month and be billed just $4.99 per book in the U.S. or $5.74 per book in Canada. That's a savings of at least 12% off the cover price! It's quite a bargain! Shipping and handling is just 50¢ per book in the U.S. and $1.25 per book in Canada.* I understand that accepting the 2 free books and gifts places me under no obligation to buy anything. I can always return a shipment and cancel at any time. The free books and gifts are mine to keep no matter what I decide.

235/335 HDN GNMP

Name (please print)

Address   Apt. #

City   State/Province   Zip/Postal Code

Email: Please check this box ☐ if you would like to receive newsletters and promotional emails from Harlequin Enterprises ULC and its affiliates. You can unsubscribe anytime.

Mail to the **Harlequin Reader Service:**
IN U.S.A.: P.O. Box 1341, Buffalo, NY 14240-8531
IN CANADA: P.O. Box 603, Fort Erie, Ontario L2A 5X3

Want to try 2 free books from another series! Call 1-800-873-8635 or visit www.ReaderService.com.

HSE21R2